Saved

Denali M. Pinto

Saved

ISBN: 150030199X

ISBN-13: 978-1500301996

DEDICATION

I dedicate this book to my Mom and Dad. You guys are the best. You both always help me get through the toughest times. You both also helped me a ton with this novel. I could not have done this without you. I love you guys.

Saved

CONTENTS

Saved

ACKNOWLEDGMENTS

Thank you to my awesome eighth grade Advanced Language Arts teacher, Mr. Oberndorf for giving me this assignment. He really inspired me to write my novel. Thank you to my amazing Grandma Linda. She gave me great ideas and kept encouraging me to write more. Thank you to my Mom and Dad. You both helped me edit my novel which greatly helped me to get the editing part done. Thank you to my brother, Brody. You are the most amazing brother ever. I am so thankful that you helped me to edit my novel.

Saved

PROLOGUE

It all started when the radiation hit. It wiped out our world as we know it. Now all we have left are a few safe houses. Many of us changed, mankind fell to the radiation, turning mutant. Now all that is left is the Resistance: just a few of us who will do anything that we can to fight back. That's what we do, we fight. My name is Caleb Hanson. I was part of an elite group of fighters, we were called the Rangers and we were the best of the Resistance fighters.

Those of us who fell to the radiation have turned into non-human creatures, animals or "bugs" as we call them. Bugs do everything they can to destroy us and the Resistance. We think that they are in a trance. The Resistance and its leaders all believe that there is a way to save them. We are just trying to figure out how. We can capture them and experiment on them. All we know is that they are getting more and more powerful. They are getting stronger, trying to break our never-faltering grasp on what was left of the world.

Our missions were going well. We were getting good at defeating them, finding lots of information and finding new ways to defeat them. The Ranger's main mission was trying to figure out who was controlling the bugs. The Ranger's mission was to figure out what creature was making the bugs turn against us. We were accomplishing a lot, until a very important mission went very wrong.

We were going in on a standard mission. It was not a very hard mission, ranked a category 2. There were ten of us going in quietly, in a small squad. Our mission was to capture a standard mutant bug. We were closing in on our destination, only about 100 meters away. Then the leader of our group held up his hand, sensing something. I lifted my nose into the air, there, a little scent of something larger, something we were not expecting. On my helmet intercom I heard my leader's voice, calm, yet demanding, "Abort mission, I repeat, abort mission!"

That's when it hit. The beast seemed to fall from the sky. Over my intercom I heard one of my crewmate's yell.

"Holy-" he yelled, before he was cut short by an ear piercing sound.

It was a sharp cry as if to call another beast. I was breathing hard, my breath was fogging up my mask and a rush of adrenaline was pulsing through my body. I saw the bug, the object that we were coming for, and looked at my scanner. I could get to the bug if I went now.

Nearby my crewmates were firing at the beast. My leader was yelling to leave. There was panic. I could feel the chaotic scrambling to get away.

All I saw was the bug. It was only about 50 meters away from me now. I could still get to the bug. I started out at a run, gradually turning to a full sprint. I was closing in, 30 meters. My breath was fogging up my mask. 20 meters, I could still make it, 10, my heart was pumping with adrenaline, but I was almost there. The bug bared its teeth at me.

That's when it happened. The bug morphed into a creature unlike any bug that I have ever seen. My suit scanner told me that I was fighting an old animal called a cat, but not just any cat, a leopard. My suit transformed to match the skills of a cat. I jumped and met the bug in the air, battling with it until we reached the ground. The cat had quick reflexes. It lashed out fast and hit me. From there I pulled out my favorite weapon that I could use on a bug.

"Taser!" I yelled. I pulled the ball-like taser from my belt. Then, I saw my chance. As the bug fought, it attacked with its left and then parried with its right. I faked to the left. Then, I threw the taser down onto the bug's body. Its flesh rippled and then it went still.

A cold silence came across the night. All I heard was my ragged breathing and my heart pounding so loudly that it sounded like it was going to break free. I turned slowly and saw the large beast. The beast was no more than 150 meters away. It was eyeing me up, preparing to attack.

Scales cascaded down its body. This beast was a quadruped. It was one of the most dangerous animals, to be mutated, on the planet. This beast was part mountain lion-part shark but it did not need water to breath. Its breath came out as a small cloud in the cold night.

From this far away I could hear it growling. I could see the pure evil in its eyes.

Pushing a button on my black suit I put my wrist to my mouth, taking only slow movements. Into my intercom I spoke, "I have the bug. I repeat I have the bug."

From the other side, "Good work, where is your leader?"

I vaguely remembered the yelling. I remembered the beast grabbing a Ranger and throwing him to the ground. I remembered the beast screaming. I remembered how loud and high pitched the scream was. I remembered my leader yelling to abort the mission. I remembered chaos and panic. I remembered the beast taking them out. I remembered them all gone.

"Ranger, Where is your leader?" The Resistance asked again.

I took a deep breath before responding, "My leader is dead, one confirmed survivor, me, you need to get me out of here, now!" I spoke in a demanding voice into the intercom, just as the beast began to charge.

Its scales rippled back with every step it took giving it a dragon-like look. Its sharp teeth were pulled back in a snarl. I got down on one knee taking out my long distance sniper. The beast charged.

It was fast and I knew that I couldn't outrun it. I fired. The bullet hit the beast in the thigh. The beast faltered but kept running. I knew that I needed to get out of there as fast as I could.

From the other side of my intercom the Resistance spoke. "Ok, we are giving you a rider. It should come up on your screen right about now."

On my mask I saw a picture of a type of motorcycle. It had two thick wheels, one in the front of the bike and the other in the back of the bike. Below the picture it showed MAX SPEED 200 miles/ hour. Then a button started blinking on my suit. I touched it and the rider came up a few meters away. I grabbed the bug and threw it on the back of the rider. Its limp body fell over the back seat.

The beast was closing in on me. My helmet scanner was blinking red. 50 meters, the beast was getting closer, picking up speed. I could hear the thumping of his feet hitting the hard ground. I swung my sniper over my shoulder and sprinted to the rider. The beast was getting closer, 20 meters. I hopped on the rider and took off just as the beast reached me. It jumped into the air and caught my left shoulder, ripping into my flesh.

I yelled in pain and lost control of the rider, it spun out from under me and I fell to the ground rolling before getting back into a fighting position. The mutated animals had adapted, but so had we.

The beast jumped for me again. This time I met it in the air. My fist closed into a ball and spikes then sprouted from my suit's knuckles. I smashed my fist into the beast's face and my knuckles erupted in pain.

The scales on the beast's body had closed into protective body armor making it impossible to penetrate its skin, though my hand was on fire. My strength had made the beast fall to ground. I fell too, but was quick to get back up. The beast had gotten up even faster, it dove into me again, but this time as it jumped, time seemed to slow.

I saw all of the beast's injuries, where I should hit it to win. I saw where its armor faltered and knew where it was going to hit me next. I looked into the beasts eyes and saw nothing but despair. I was lying on the ground. My back was resting against the ground's cool surface. I felt the cool ground. I smelled sweat and heat. The beast leaped. I could see where he was going to come up short and where his claws would grab once he hit me.

I grabbed my sword and slid forward, under the beast's legs. While doing this I held my sword in front of me, my sword ripped into the beast's flesh cutting his underbelly, one of its only soft spots. The beast had so much momentum that it staked himself. I then hopped up to my feet and sprang onto the beast's back. I found the soft spot in the quadruped's shoulder. Then I stabbed. The beast screamed in agony, and then it went still.

I sat there for a moment, on the now dead beast's back. I sat there not feeling, not moving, and not thinking. I sat there and awaited the pain.

"Ranger, are you okay?" There was silence, "Ranger, do you copy."

"Resistance, I copy. The beast is defeated, I am alive." That's when I fell off the beast, falling onto the ground with a thud. I was out cold.

CHAPTER 1

"Caleb Hanson, please report to the general's office as soon as possible. Caleb Hanson, please report the general's office as soon as possible." I had just sat down to my sandwich and soup.

"Good luck man." I looked down at the guy who spoke. He looked older than me, and he gave me a sympathetic look.

"Thanks." I stood up leaving my tray behind and walked, with my head up, out of the cafeteria. I knew that I was going to be called down eventually. It was one month after the Rangers were wiped out and I was still in shock. I had no idea what the head generals were going to do.

They were in complete control of the situation and for once in my life I felt hopeless. In a fight there are always situations that put you in a bad position but there is always a way to turn the fight around and take victory. Right now I had no idea what they would do to me. I expected the worst.

I walked down a long hallway toward the generals offices. I was meeting them in the main office room. I saw the large door of the main office.

The wood of the door was dark brown and it was taller than my six foot three inches. I ran my hand through my dirty blond hair.

As I reached for the door my heart seemed to catch in my throat. I thought back to all that happened that night one month ago. I remembered seeing the quadruped fall from the sky. I remembered being alone.

The memory of facing the beast came back to me. I remembered getting hit. I remembered finally taking the beast down. After that, I lost memory.

It all seemed to go by in a blur. I remembered voices, waking up on an operation table with surgeons surrounding me. I remembered the feeling of pain in my shoulder and passing out again. Then, I remembered waking up on a bed. I was surrounded by white.

That moment was when I remembered the feeling, the feeling of being alone. I pushed those thoughts out of my mind and knocked loudly on the door.

From inside I heard an old man's gravelly voice, "Come in."

I pushed the door open ready to face what might be my last day in the field, to my last day as a fighter. As soon as I stepped in the room I almost stepped back in surprise. The whole committee was there. They all looked at me with interest except the general who was frowning as he leaned back in his chair. His eyes seemed to be trying to bore into me. The general looked at me. There was no happiness in his eyes. His name was General Daniels. He had been the general ever since my father had…

"Sit down, Hanson." The statement was a command and I sat down immediately, never taking my eyes off of the general. "Why do you think we have called you here?"

The question surprised me and my composure faltered. Then I regained it, realizing that he was curious. General Daniels had leaned forward in his chair. His hands rested in an arch below his chin.

"I am sure that being called down has something to do with the event that took place no more than a month ago." The general leaned back in his chair a look of satisfaction replaced his curiosity.

"Do you remember anything from that night?" One man on the committee questioned. He seemed to be puzzled.

"Not much."

"Hanson, we are impressed with what you did that night. No other one man had been able to take down a quadruped. Let alone a 17 year old boy taking down a mountain lion shark," General Daniels paused, "The way you took that beast down…"

The general faltered, he was looking at my face, trying to see an expression that might give my thoughts away. He thought that I was hiding something from that night. I kept my face blank, trying not to show emotion.

"Hanson, we are giving you a new position. You have been repositioned to a new group. You will go to their training practices and work with them. You will obey their leader's commands. You are now part of their group."

A wave of dismay washed through me. The general knew that I didn't want to be repositioned but he knew what was best for me. He knew that I should be promoted. I could tell that he knew that it wasn't the right decision by the way his fists clenched when he spoke those words. At the same time, I saw the edge that had been in his eyes when I sat down was now gone.

Now it was replaced by a look of satisfaction. My muscles tensed. What was behind the general's decision? Was someone or something standing in the way, was he? I forced myself to smile, looking the general right in the eye.

"You are dismissed." I stood, running my hand through my hair.

"Sir?" The general looked up. "What group am I going to be repositioned to?"

The general paused but he forced himself to speak, "You are repositioned to the Terminators. You will meet with them in the morning. You may go."

I stood, and left the room.

CHAPTER 2

The beast was chasing me. It was unlike any beast that I had ever seen before. It had a muzzle-like face with a long tail. Its body was covered in fur and its legs and forearms were long and large, about the size of me. It had two rows of sharp canine teeth. The tail had a rattle-like object on the end and I could hear it rattling. It was fast, running on all fours. Its large feet hit the ground one at a time: thud, thud, thud, thud, pause, thud, thud, thud...

My feet pounded the ground, I had no weapons on me and the beast was closing in, never letting me catch my breath. That's when I heard it, the sound of water, and a lot of it.

The water had the sound of an echo, as if it was rushing into a large cavern or pit. I wasn't paying attention to where I was going.

All I heard was the thud, thud, thud, thud of the beast closing in behind me. My feet touched the gravelly ground and before me I saw the rock fall away. I slid to a stop right before the top of a cliff.

Looking down more than 500 meters, I saw water was pouring around me from all sides, where the rivers met the cliff. I was trapped. Behind me, I heard ragged breathing. The beast had stopped running and was looking me up and down. It knew that it had me at last. I could tell that it knew, too.

I could tell that it wanted to savor me. I had been hard to catch but now he had me. He had me on the top of the cliff with nowhere else to go. I was trapped. I was stuck. There was no way out.

The beast growled. As it did so it showed of its sharp teeth. The beast showed its teeth that were prepared and made for one reason only: to rip and to tear. A wave of fear washed through me, a fear that I could not control. Then, anger.

The anger was so great that all I saw was red, red that outlined the beast. The anger was uncontrollable. It was so fierce that I was shocked. The beast sensed a change in my attitude and it snarled wanting to sense my fear again. It took a step closer and my anger grew. I wanted to take the beast down.

Then I remembered, on the edge of my memory, something special, something more. There was a thought that my mind could not grasp. A memory. I knew that it was something special, something hidden. This thought was something that my brain wanted to retrieve. Suddenly, without thinking, without knowing, I turned. I ran at full speed and jumped off the cliff.

"Caleb, Caleb! Wake up." I snapped awake. All I remembered was falling, falling down a long way and anger, anger so great that it was uncontrollable.

I tried to focus. I was confused, angry, and scared. My fear was so great that it overpowered the rest. I slumped in my bed, and my shoulders sagged.

"Caleb, what's wrong?" I looked up into the face of the young man in front of me.

"Justin," my body relaxed, "what's going on out there?" I looked at the door of our dormitory.

"We are on lockdown alert-" Justin's eyebrows furrowed together.

"What?"

"Yeah, there… there is a beast in the Resistance." Justin's worried expression for me changed into one of concern for the Resistance, "General ordered all pre-officers to stay in their dorms with doors locked, we are not supposed to let anyone in, they are afraid that someone let the beast in."

"What class break-in is this?" I said, cutting Justin off. Justin paused as if not sure to tell me or not, "Justin, what class break-in is this?" I asked again.

"This is a class 5 break-in." Justin said finally. My body

reacted before my brain even fully processed this. A memory came back to me. This time it came easily, almost too easily. It flowed into my mind.

I remembered a face. Then, I remembered loud noises. I remembered voices that came into our house. They were hard to hear because of the static. I remember looking up into a face like my own.

It had green eyes and short blond hair. The face turned into an expression of pain. Then, it left. The man ran out of the room. There was a gun on his back. I remember my mom's face. It held an expression of pain and disbelief. I remember hearing more voices on the intercom, "This is a class 5 break-in, I repeat. This is a class 5 break-in." Then I remember the lights going out and the screaming.

I was breathing heavy again, leaning over the side of my bed. I heard a voice.

"Caleb, what's going on? Caleb?" The voice sounded too much like my father's. My hand grasped the chain around my neck. My body relaxed immediately. I opened my eyes. Justin was standing in front of me, his expression was worried.

"I'm okay," I breathed. This was not the first time that I had had a flashback to my father. I knew that it was not going to be the last. "Justin I can't just wait-" He cut me off, a smile stretched across his face.

"We are not going to. Suit up!"

We were in the hallway leading to the stairs. Justin and I were making our way down the hallway. I could hear his heavy breathing through our suit's intercoms. We hadn't been able to do it alone.

"Okay, I can see the beast. He's on the second floor left wing. Do not use the right stairs!" A voice came through our intercoms. This voice was coming from our dormmate, Troy. He was a standard computer geek and hacker and our home base operator.

"Copy that," Justin's smooth voice came out easily, he was relaxed. His body posture told me that he was ready for anything. He knew the consequences if we got caught and he was willing to accept them for me. For me. I thought back to the beast in my dream. Class 5 break-in, Justin and I were going to take this beast down.

"Get off the floor that you are on, now." I heard the voice of Troy, he sounded demanding. "There are officials on your floor. They cannot know that you are out of your rooms."

Justin and I took off down the hall. "There will be a chute to your left. Take it, now!" I hopped in. I fell for a moment before I touched ground. I landed softly on the hard floor. Justin followed close behind, doing the same. "Okay, you are in one of the storage rooms. The exit is on the west side wall, closest to the gun rack. To exit you must lift up the handle and pull back." There was a pause. "You are clear, leave now." Justin sprinted to the door and threw up the handle. I followed close behind.

We glanced down the long corridor and saw nothing. There was a pause on Troy's end and then a quick intake of breath. "You guys are being followed." Troy said those words as a fact.

"What?" I turned around, "By the beast?"

"No, no, no by some sort of human, I can't get a reading on his status or ranking though."

"Troy, where is the beast?" Justin's smooth voice cut through Troy's rambling. There was a pause. "Troy! Where is the beast?" Justin's voice was demanding this time.

My blood went cold as Troy gasped and then spoke, the words came out slowly and carefully as if they might startle. "The beast is right behind you."

A chill went through my body as I heard the breathing, the loud huffs, and then the growling.

"We will take him together," Justin's hushed voice whispered in my ear. "Turn slowly, now." We both turned around and I was not at all surprised at what I saw. The beast was huge, about 7 feet tall. Its front legs were about as big as me and the back legs were twice that size.

The beast had a muzzle-shaped face and huge teeth, dripping with saliva. And there was the tail. It was very long and there was a rattle attached to the end. Every instinct in my body told me to run. But I held my ground knowing that the beast was much faster than me.

"Now," Justin spoke and I leaped into the air. I took the

right side, while Justin took the left. The beast whipped its tail at Justin and hit him hard across the chest. I saw Justin crumple, his body was no match for the beast's strength. Justin fell to the ground hard.

That gave me time. I hit its shoulder with my blade and dragged downward ripping into its flesh. The beast howled in pain and I hopped back just as it lunged for the spot where I used to be. He got nothing but air.

To the side of me Justin was still on the ground. I took out my knives, one of my favorite weapons, just as the beast looked at me again. I could see the hatred and despise in his eyes. My blood was pumping more. I remembered that past night, a hand in my own. No. I had to stay in this moment. My hand gripped the handle of the knife, and I refocused.

I threw the knife from my right hand like a baseball pitcher. It was accurate, hitting the beast in its right shoulder. The already-wounded shoulder was dripping with blood. The knife lodged itself in the beast's right shoulder and the beast roared in pain. I then threw the knife from my left hand, this one side-armed. It hit the beast in the chest. The knife lodged right as the beast began to run.

The beast screamed in pain again but kept charging. I then took out my doubled-sided blade, my cutlass, and sprinted at the beast.

Right before we met, the beast jumped. This completely surprised me. I reacted to its move and I slid, trying to get underneath the beast. But my reaction was too late. One of the beast's claws dug into my left leg. I felt it rip into my flesh tearing into me. I yelled in pain.

The pain was like what I had never experienced before. It was blinding, but my adrenaline and anger toward the beast overpowered the pain. I rolled to my feet in a hunched battle position. Then I stood.

The beast turned around. My knives were still sticking out of it, lodged deeply into its skin. Its left shoulder was bleeding. I grabbed my cutlass more lightly, this time ready for the beast to charge. It did. The beast was mad at me now. I had been too hard to kill. I sprinted at it taking four steps and then jumped into the air. Before I knew it I was flying over the beast. I angled my sword downward so that as I flew over the beast the sword dug into its flesh, ripping into the fur on its back.

It slowed to a stop. The beast was bleeding all over now. I walked over to it, slicing its chest one last time. It fell to the ground. Its large head smacked against the floor hard before it was still. Before I knew it I was on top of the beast. I took my cutlass and I set it in the mode to make it into two halves, a blade on each half. Then, I stabbed the beast again, one half in each side of its large head.

I wanted to be sure that the beast was dead. I never wanted the beast to ever wake up. I wanted to do it for my father. I wanted the beast dead for the memory of my father. I wanted it dead for the life of my father. I felt myself shaking. My hands were shaking uncontrollably.

I crawled over to Justin, who was unconscious on the ground and fell on top of him. I lay there for a moment just as the officers busted into the hallway. They had their guns ready. They were preparing to corner the beast.

All they saw was the large beast. It was lying, dead, on the ground. They also saw me. I was lying over Justin. I could feel the blood pumping through my body.

I could see the officers faintly. They were dressed in all white. I could vaguely see them tearing down the hallway toward us. I could feel the beast on the ground beside me and Justin, too. I smiled realizing what I had done, what we had done. My vision grew even more blurry. As soon as the first white official reached me, I passed out.

CHAPTER 3

"We're busted. We are totally busted."

"Troy, I know! For the millionth time *we* are not busted: only Justin and I are busted. Let it go. We know how much trouble we are in. We knew how much trouble we were going to get in. Now stop worrying."

"I knew that I shouldn't have let you guys go. It was too dangerous."

"Troy!" I stopped lifting, setting the bench press down with a thud. I sat up, taking a deep breath before continuing, "Troy-"

"And now you are lifting again! Think of your shoulder," Troy stammered. At that comment I rolled my shoulder back feeling the tightness and soreness of the muscle.

"It helps me get it loose again." I paused, choosing my words carefully. "What happened that night," I sighed, remembering what happened that night, "is in the past. We are now part of the future. Justin and I took down a class 5 beast. The committee will have to take that into consideration when judging what to do with us."

"Something bad is going to happen. You guys are going to have to stop fighting. They are going to pull you from the training school that you are in. You're not going to be able to fight anymore."

"Troy, they would never pull fighters with our skill out of the training school. Their goal is to take the best fighters, not get rid of them." Shooting pain went through my shoulder and I gasped in pain, then I took deep breaths.

I was okay. A face flashed into my mind. It was Dad's face, much like my own. He was smiling, congratulating me. He patted me on the back. I could feel his hand there. I opened my eyes and felt myself smiling.

"Caleb, are you okay?" Troy's worried voice pulled me out of my memory, bringing me back to consciousness. "Caleb-"

A woman from the committee stepped into the room. I watched as she started scanning the weight room for something or someone.

She was wearing her graying hair up tight in a bun. I could see how tightly it was pulled. The way she held herself, upright and rigid made me think that she was nervous.

Finally, her dark brown eyes found mine. I could see her gasp a little. She started making her way over to me. As she passed others, she never took her eyes off of mine.

Her footsteps were small and she needed many of them to carry her across the small room.

When she reached me she took a deep breath before she spoke. She spoke loudly and she sounded very confident in herself. "Mr. Hanson, General Daniels would like to see you," she paused, when she did not see any movement from me she added, "immediately." I could hear the dismay in her voice.

I looked at Troy. His eyes looked nervous. They were full of shame as well. I sighed.

"Please come immediately, Mr. Hanson." Her voice was full of distress. I could see that pieces of hair from her tight bun were starting to fall out.

I stood up. Her body seemed so small and frail when I stood. I towered over her.

"Alright, I'm ready, let's go." I heard Troy gasp softly. I looked down at him and smiled.

"Good," her voice was crisp and stern, "Right this way, Mr. Hanson." I set my jaw straight and followed her out of the weight room. I followed her to the general. I followed her to what might be my last time to ever hold my cutlass in my hand and take out a beast.

"Caleb Hanson," General Daniels was standing at his

window when I entered the room, "that was very kind of you to come with Mrs. Fredrick without a fuss. You can tell how stressed she can get." I heard humor in his voice. However, I did not find anything that he said funny.

The general turned to me. His eyes flickered back and forth, only slightly. "You disobeyed my orders, Caleb." His eyes looked sad.

I remembered back to the day when I first found out that my father was never going to come back. I remembered back to when I first found out that my father was dead.

General Daniels had held me close. He had whispered in my ear and told me that everything would be okay. He had sounded so reassuring that I believed him. I believed that everything would be okay.

As I looked at General Daniels now I did not see the reassuring man that I had seen that past night. Instead, I saw a man that was blind to what I could do. He knew that I could help him fight the beasts. Why did he keep punishing me for what I had done to help?

I felt myself start to get angry. Why was the general doing this to me?

The general continued speaking, "I have to tell you, Caleb, I am very impressed." The general smiled but the smile did not reach his eyes. I could tell that he was lying. He was getting good at it, but the lie was there.

"I am impressed but you did not listen to my orders. I am afraid that I have to punish you. If I do not then the others may be misguided into thinking that what you did was okay.

"Don't get me wrong, Caleb, you have a talent like no other. However, other kids your age do not have the same skill. So, I am demoting you." There was false sadness in the general's voice. I could tell that he was glad of his decision. I could see some of the stress fade away from his eyes.

He wanted to get me out of the way, but why?

"You are dismissed, Caleb." I stood and watched as General Daniels turned back to the window.

I could not help myself, I had to ask. "Why, Sir?" The general turned again, this time I could see some anger in his eyes, "Sir, you know that I am one of the best. You know that I am great for my age. Why are you doing this to me?"

The general sounded furious when he spoke again, "I have made my decision Mr. Hanson, you must obey."

"So you don't have a good reason," I could not help myself. All of the anger that I had been feeling for the past years started spilling out, "why do you think that you have this power over me? General Daniels, you will never be my father. You will never be like him."

I heard General Daniels take an intake of breath. I saw his face turn a pale white.

"That is enough, Mr. Hanson. Security please escort Mr. Hanson from the room!" The general yelled. I could tell that the general was furious. His eyes blazed and his hands were balled into fists.

Two men walked in and grabbed my arms. I let them pull me away. But not before I spoke again. I hoped that the general heard my words. I hoped that he heard them and listened. I hoped that for once in his life, he acted.

"You are a coward, General Daniels. You are nothing but a coward." I watched as the general turned his back to me. He continued to look back out of the window. His two bodyguards threw me out of the room.

I felt myself step into my dormitory. Justin still was not there. I guess that he was still in the infirmary. Troy was there. He looked up at me. I saw the hope in his eyes. I also saw the sadness. I turned away from him.

I made my way over to my bed and sat down. The comforter did not feel comfortable. To me, it felt like a lie, a lie that the general was hiding under, a lie that was built from a coward.

Troy did not speak, but I did not want him to. I leaned back onto my pillow and closed my eyes.

I felt a flashback coming on and let it. I let the memory take over me. I felt myself sinking into the memory.

We were outside, the sun was shining bright. Only, it was not my father. It was my grandfather. He was sitting on a wooden bench. His face was angled upward towards the sun. He wore a large smile.

I was sitting beside him. I had a book open and was trying to read. The sun kept getting in my way. I wanted to get up and move around. I wanted to run.

"You must read, Caleb." It was as if my grandfather had sensed my frustration. It was as if he knew that I wanted to get up and run.

"Why, Grandfather? Why do I have to read?" I looked up at my grandfather's face.

He opened his eyes and looked at me. I could see the amusement on his features.

"You must read because you have to know how to calm your body's desire to move. In a battle there will be moments when calm means everything. You must learn how to gain control and be calm."

I felt myself sigh. I looked back at the book. The words were so small. I listened to my grandfather's words and read.

I opened my eyes.

Troy was sitting across the room. He was doing work on his computer.

I stood and made my way toward the door. Troy looked up from his work.

"Where are you going?" He asked. He sounded suspicious.

"I have to see my grandfather."

"What? But Caleb-"

"I have to see him." I turned from Troy and walked out the door.

At the air train stop everyone was looking at me. They were all just staring. None of them were looking away. The whispers were starting up. All I could do was stand there and act like I didn't know what they were looking at.

I looked at my watch. The air train should be here any second now. It should come. I bounced on the soles of my feet waiting for the air train so that I could escape these unwanted stares.

The air train finally came. It slid gracefully to a stop beside the platform. I stepped on as the doors closed behind me. I stepped into a seat near the doors. Into my seat speaker I spoke clearly. "Residents Community,"

The computer in my seat spoke back, "Which region?"

"Outer Region, Near City Hall Province," on my computer screen a map showed me the layout of the Resistance, stretched across North America. All of the Resistances other than the North American Resistance had fallen.

The second strongest had been the African Resistance. They had fallen about two years ago. Now, anywhere you go besides North America is infested with beasts, bugs, and air not suitable for human health. At least, that is what we have been told. Now, I was not sure what else our Resistance and general had been lying about.

My computer showed a blinking light near the East Coast Region, right on the ocean. I tapped it, that's where my grandfather had wanted to live.

He loved the ocean and the noise that it made. It reminded him of my father, of me. A red dot showed where I was. I was currently in the Colorado region. There were no beaches or lakes here. Colorado was a desert. This meant that it was infested with beasts. Bugs were scarce in my region. Bug liked the cool and wet places.

"5 hour fly." My computer said as the air train took off from the platform.

"Please enjoy nice cool refreshing drinks from our home of Colorado!" A women's voice came through the computer, "these drinks are made high up in the Rocky Mountains, try one now." I turned off my computer screen, turning the ad off with it.

Leaning onto my side, I realized that I couldn't remember how long it had been since I had seen my grandfather. I closed my eyes, this time drifting into a dreamless sleep.

"Grandfather, how old were you when you took down your first category 5 beast?"

"I don't know, probably 14 or 15." Grandfather's face was unreadable, his eyes twinkled but his face was impassive. I couldn't tell if he was lying or not.

"Really?" I asked, suspicious.

"No, Caleb," he laughed, "I was nowhere near as young as you, I was definitely an officer, so probably around 23. That was the first one that I took down myself."

I sighed, remembering the night with the Rangers. "How did the beast kill all the Rangers? How come it could kill all of them but it couldn't kill me?"

"Now, those questions probably have something to do with fear." Grandfather paused before he continued. "I'm guessing your other group mates had never seen a quadruped before. I'm guessing that they had no idea what to expect."

"But my leader must have seen one before. He must have fought one. I thought that his job was to not fear, to be a rock, to have a solid core."

"Maybe those characteristics escaped him when he saw everyone dying, he just wasn't prepared."

"But grandfather, none of us were prepared. We were not prepared for the break-in either."

"You must have a stronger heart than the rest of them. You know how it feels." With this sentence he reached forward and patted my chest. I nodded at his words, his hand moved over to my shoulder. "What is wrong with your shoulder?"

"Last night..." I faltered, not sure what to say.

"Is Justin alright?"

"Yes, he got out of the hospital today."

"Good," grandfather leaned back in his chair as a ding sounded in the kitchen. "My dinner's ready." Grandfather had a happy expression on his face. "I ordered for you tonight as well, I had a feeling you would come."

I smiled and walked over to the kitchen. In the delivery slot were two meals, one for grandfather labeled, Albert Hanson, and the other was labeled Caleb Hanson. I smiled when I saw what he had ordered me.

He ordered one of my favorite meals, roasted salmon with buttered noodles and a side salad. Grandfather's meal wasn't much different. Tonight he had ordered a pesto dish served with chicken and bread. I brought the dishes over to the dining room turning on the television as I passed by.

"Many of our parents are worried for our children." The news reporter spoke, the cafeteria for the Resistance was behind her. “Many people feel that training our children at our training facilities is no longer safe. This is now the second beast break-in in our community. Many people are thinking that they should be putting trained officers stationed outside of the school building and on all paths leading to the school. What do you think Mike? Is there a security risk?”

“I don’t know, Cheryl.” The camera went to the man standing beside Cheryl, his face looked concerned. “It seems like the school could have better security. With our kids being trained well and learning, we don’t want to take away from their learning experience.”

“That’s true, Mike.” Cheryl looked back at the camera. “Please stay tuned to who took down the beast and how, after the break.” The camera broke away to an advertisement and I looked at my grandfather.

“Grandfather?” I rested his dinner down at the table and set mine beside his.

“Hmm?” he asked curiously, digging into his noodle dish.

“Why have there been,” I paused, “two break-ins into our Resistance? I did not think that it would happen again.”

Grandfather paused, debating my question. “My guess is that whoever is controlling the beasts has finally figured out where we are training our children.

“I bet you that this species is as strong and as smart as, probably even smarter than humans. Now they are going to keep attacking our community more and more because now they know our weakness.”

“So you think that there is a higher power?”

“I am sure of it.”

“How are you so sure?”

“The way that the beasts are acting, the spots that bugs have been found, the way that beast came out of nowhere when your last group, the Rangers, was so close to finding that bug, the way that now beasts have been breaking into your school, everything adds up, there is most definitely a higher power. Since we have not been to other countries in years those countries are probably where the beast leaders have set up camp.”

“Why don’t we go back out to the other countries?” I was confused. If we had an idea to where the leaders of the beasts were, why didn't we investigate?

"Fear," grandfather stated without a pause, "The authorities are afraid. They just want to sit and hide. I have known for some time, but now, if we do not take action with this latest break in, it is time for a new committee."

"Is that why the general did not promote me? Did he think that I would gain too much power and then lead my own expeditions without his consent?"

"That is definitely one of the reasons." Grandfather smiled.

"Why?" I was angry now, and grandfather's smile quickly faded. "Before this moment I had always looked up to the general, sort of like a third father." My father…

I was sitting on a swing. I was a child, no more than six years old. The swing chains were cold. I was wearing a hat and a warm jacket, but no gloves. Then I heard a voice, "Caleb, you must not let go of the chains, think of the feel of them now, feel the coldness on your hands?" I nodded, "Good, remember that feeling. Now think that your life is in those chains, that you cannot let go, and if you do, you might not see another day."

I listened to his words carefully, taking in every last detail, every last sound. "You might be in a situation like this sometime in your life. Just remember, don't let go of the chains." I looked up but all I saw were two hands gripping my back strongly. I felt safe and secure sitting there with those hands on my back, two strong hands holding me there, right there on the swing. They were never going to let go.

Just like me, I was never going to let go. I remembered his words. *Do not let go, do not let go.* Do not let-

"Caleb, are you alright? Caleb!"

My eyes snapped open, and I found my hands clutching the countertop so tightly that my knuckles were turning white. I released my grip on the granite counter and slouched back in my chair.

"Caleb?" I looked into the green eyes of my grandfather, so much like mine, so much like my father's. My father's words *do not let go.* I took a deep breath as if to rid my mind of my thoughts. "Caleb?"

"I'm okay," I breathed, and spoke quietly, "I just had a…"

"Memory?" Grandfather asked a quiet question to his

voice.

I nodded my head slowly, taking time to savor this moment with my grandfather. “Grandfather? Have they ever happened to you, these, memories, about,” I paused, “dad?”

Grandfather leaned his head back in his chair, as if deep in thought. “Yes,” he said softly. “Ever since…” Grandfather’s voice trailed off.

“That night?” I asked.

“Yes, the night of the first break-in.” grandfather looked at me hard, his bright green eyes looked right into my soul, as if he could tell what I was thinking, “Caleb, you’re father’s death was not your fault,” I felt tears brim into my eyes, my father…

“Caleb, look at me,” grandfather's voice was stern, and I let my eyes meet with his, “We both blame ourselves for your father’s death. It was not your fault, nor was it was mine.” Grandfather took a deep breath, and then continued, “Your father would be very proud if he saw you now, he would be very proud.”

I looked into grandfather's eyes and saw a piece of myself hidden in there, as well as a piece of my father. I threw myself into my grandfather’s arms and hugged him hard. I felt his arms go around me. We sat there for a moment, taking in the memory. At last, he pulled away from our embrace.

“Caleb, you are not a coward, you are a hero. I know what you will try to do. You want to figure out how to end this, this state that Earth and the Resistance are in. You want to try to stop it all, on your own. You can’t. On your own you cannot do this. You must have a group of at least thirty others. The head general will not have your back. He will not support you and he may try to do everything he can to stop you. He does not want the public to think that a 17 year old boy can lead this great of an expedition by himself. But Caleb, you can. You are strong enough inside and have the perfect skills, the skills of a leader. You will be greater than me, greater than your father, and Caleb, you will be strong.

“Do you still have the chain that your father gave to you?”

“Yes.” I grabbed the chain that hung around my neck, feeling the smooth but hard texture underneath my skin, just like the swing chain, *do not let go*, I could hear my father’s voice inside my head, *do not let go*.

“Good,” grandfather said, “Caleb, whatever happens out

there, I'm very proud of you. Now go do what you know how to do best. Go and lead your troops into the regions that have been unexplored for decades.

"Caleb?" Grandfather looked into my eyes one last time. Our green eyes met, so similar, so alike. "This mission cannot fail. This is a category 10 mission. In this mission you will save the world." I nodded. Grandfather's leader-like qualities took its toll on me as he spoke to me this time.

"Yes, Sir."

CHAPTER 4

"I'm ready, I can go with you." Justin winced in pain as he leaned forward. His head was so close to mine that our foreheads were almost touching. As much as I loved how earnest Justin was, I knew that I had to turn him down.

"Justin, you can't-" He cut me off again.

"I'm going. The doctor said that I can go back into training tomorrow, that I will be able to fight tomorrow. No matter what you say I'm going. There is no stopping me." I looked away, I couldn't let him come. I felt Justin's hand on my shoulder. "You're like my little brother, dude. There is no way that I'm going to let you out there alone." Justin leaned forward wincing in pain as he did so. "You can't stop me."

"Justin-"

"I'm going." There was such fierceness in his eyes that it struck me in that moment that he could be a leader easily. His sharp features were stern, high cheekbones and black short cut hair. His dark brown eyes looked at me with such intensity that I had to look away.

"Fine," I said, I could feel my body relax greatly just by saying that word. Justin relaxed too, he slumped back in his chair and leaning his head back, a satisfied look gleamed in his eyes, a look of mischief as well.

"I was hoping that you would say that." Justin's eyes gleamed. "I have already prepared a group for you, they are called the Exterminators. If we go now, we can catch them in session.

They are a fighting group, much like the Rangers, and I think that they will be perfect for your expedition. Their leader is Brendon Jones." Justin said happily. I smiled. Jones was a good leader and fighter.

"Attention!" all 40 Exterminators put their hands behind their backs and looked at their leader.

"Yes, Sir!" They all yelled in unison.

"This is Caleb Hanson." All of their eyes turned to look at me, their faces showed curiosity but most of all admiration. I looked at each and every one of them making eye contact with all of them.

"As you all know, I am Caleb Hanson, I am the son of Wesley Hanson, our previous Lieutenant General." As I said those words all of the Exterminators bore sympathy on their faces. "There have been many territories that have not been explored for decades, for example, the Asian and Chinese Resistances. They have all fallen for over 15 years. My guess is that there is something or someone else out there that is controlling the beasts and bugs. I think that their base camp could be in one of the already-fallen Resistances. What I want to do is investigate, and try to stop whatever species that is trying to kill us."

I was using the theory that my grandfather had helped to provide for me.

"Is that how the radiation hit?" One of the Exterminators stepped forward as he spoke. He was probably about 20 and he had short brown hair and hazel eyes. He asked his question with confidence.

"My guess is a species tried to wipe us out with the radiation," the man nodded his head slowly as if processing this idea, "when it hit some of us fell to it, turning into bugs but some of us had an immune system that was strong enough to withstand the radiation, so we held our ground. Even animals were mutated and changed into 'part' creatures. Whoever was trying to wipe us out in the first place is definitely growing stronger by the years, if there is an unknown species out there it will probably be planning an attack that will completely wipe us out at any time. This time will be soon." I paused, catching my breath.

"Is this a mission that the general assigned you to lead?"

"No," I said calmly, looking the man who asked the question right in the eye. "The general does not know that I am planning to lead this mission. It is a category 10 mission. Many of us will not come back alive. You do not have to come if you do not want to, but if you do you will be stopping what may be the apocalypse." I said this statement firmly, all of the Exterminators were looking at me right in the eye, and none of them were backing down.

"Good." I spoke loudly. I hoped that my voice was confident. "We are leaving at 11 tonight, bring everything that is necessary for a 1-3 year trip, on our way we will face dangers that have never been faced before in the history of humankind. Bring all weapons and all technology, but nothing more than you can carry. Meet on the 5th floor maintenance room. Do not tell anyone that we are leaving or that we have plans of going somewhere. Do not speak of this to anyone. If you are not in our meeting spot by 11 we will not wait for you.

"By completing this mission we will save mankind and our Resistance will grow and be strong again, but if we fail this mission mankind will be up to the fate of the world and will probably face another radiation. Are you with me!?" All of the men started yelling at the top of their lungs.

"For the Resistance!" they all screamed, "for mankind!"

I was in my dorm bathroom. It was small. My arms could stretch across the whole room, from door to shower wall if I wanted them to.

I was standing in front of the mirror. I wore my black suit. The breastplate stretched strong and smooth across my chest. The shoulder protectors stretched across my high back and connected to make a strong hold on my shoulders.

The suit was full body and stretched across my torso and down to connect smoothly with my ultra-lightweight boots. The suit was very flexible. It felt as if I was just wearing clothes, but it was as strong as steel. I held my chain hard, grasping the familiar feel, the chain texture.

Do not let go. I was never going to let go. I tucked my

chain into the breastplate of my suit.

My helmet rested on top of the sink along with my cutlass. I took the cutlass and put it on the back of my suit, where it was held in a sheath. I set my suit weapons and made sure the power was full. On my wrist a blue light blinked on, 100% full.

Flexing my fingers, gloves sprouted over them. I smiled, and walked out of my bathroom almost smashing into Justin. He was dressed similar to me, he wore his black suit but on his back was his favorite weapon, a bow. His suit was unique, giving him an unlimited supply of arrows. Justin smiled.

"Ready little bro?"

I smiled back, "Sure am."

Troy came out next. He wasn't dressed in a suit, but he had a more important job. "I'll stay here," he smiled at us. "I'll be with you guys almost every step of the way. I'll be able to see everything that both of you see and everything that you do not see. I will recharge your suits when necessary and boost up your weapons when needed. I will have your backs."

"Will you be safe here? Won't they know where to find you?"

"Yes the Resistance leaders would know where to find me if I stayed here," Troy sighed, "That's why I'm not going to stay here. Remember that secret hiding place that we found as kids? Well, slowly, I have been transferring all of our equipment to that hideout. I have all of my technology stored there, plus food and water. I'm set." Troy smiled up at me.

Then he spoke again.

"Here, I made you both one of these." Troy handed each of us a medical kit. "This kit has everything that you could imagine to need, including water purifiers and food makers. With the food makers you just open the packet and pour water into it. It doesn't matter if the water is clean because it filters it. You could even pee in it if you had to. I call these food makers portages because you can transport them anywhere and they always work. I've put in about 100 packets in each of your containers. I've also put some packets in your backpacks along with some dehydrated food. No matter what, on this journey, you will not go hungry.

"There are also emergency injectors that will work if you are poisoned by a bug or plant, including some other useful stuff.

They fit in the spot underneath your weapon holder on your suit." I hooked mine in, grateful for Troy's consideration.

"Thank you, Troy," I said, smiling.

"Let's go save the world."

"We are here in the maintenance room."

"Okay, yeah I see you, walk left. You should come across a metal beam in the ceiling." I started walking left, all of the Exterminators following close behind me. I looked up and saw the metal beam.

"Alright, I see the beam."

"Follow it all the way to the end. It should be about 10 yards." I started walking and then heard a sound, but my suit's scanner told me nothing.

"Troy, do you see anything?" I saw movement up ahead, "Troy?"

"One second, I think that I do see something. Yep, something is coming up on you. It's on your left." I whipped my head to the left. Justin stepped forward and took my right side. He knew that something was about to happen. "It's moving around your group, prepare your soldiers."

"Exterminators, there is something stalking us. Prepare yourself for an attack from any side." My voice cut through the large hollow room and the Exterminators tensed. I heard Troy's confused voice.

"What the-" Right as the beasts attacked. There were at least 20 of them falling down from the ceiling, my suit's scanner lit up, telling me what the creatures were, part ape and part tiger. "Run!" Troy screamed, "Take your troops and get out of there now!" I grabbed my cutlass and sliced an ape tiger that was advancing on me into two then I shouted at my troops.

"Follow the metal pipe!"

"Get out of here!" I turned to Justin who was fighting with me, not going with the rest of the group. "Justin, Go! Lead them!" The apes were advancing on us, "I'll be right out. Don't worry!" I had to yell over the apes screeching noises.

"I'm not leaving you!"

"They need a leader, that's you! This is an order!" I looked

Justin right in the eye and my intense expression held his. Finally, he turned away and ran after the rest of the rest of the group. I turned to face the screeching ape tigers.

One hopped up into the air, and I sliced it with one side of my cutlass. More came. I fought through them, one by one, swinging my double-sided sword around to smash the beasts. One ape tiger jumped on my back, sinking its fangs into me, and I yelled, I drove my cutlass backward, into its flesh, it fell off, then I turned and started sprinting along down the pipe, to hopefully the exit, the beasts were following, close behind, they were closing in on me.

"Troy! Are you there?" No answer, "Troy do you copy?" I was running out of metal pipe, I could see where it ended, and a wall. I kept running. "Troy!" I yelled. I had reached the wall. There was a small door about half my size. I threw it open about to sprint out of the room and nearly fell to my death. Below about 200 meters was a drop, a cliff that dropped into a river a long way down. I stepped out onto the narrow ledge between the room and the abyss.

Just as I stepped to the side the ape tigers reached me. The first few kept running at full speed leaping out of the room and falling the 100 meters, screeching all the way down. That left two, both of them slid to a halt after the ones before them flew out over the cliff. Both of them bared their fangs at me then slipped back into the room. "Troy," I tried my mouth piece. "Troy?"

Finally I got a signal. It came in crackly though as if I was in a bad signal spot, like something was messing with our gear. "Caleb, get - out - there - take - ridge - all – way - down - where - meets - surface." I started shimmying down the ridge. I made it no more than 10 meters before I saw where the ridge broke away to nothing. About 1 meter of space was between me and the other part of the ridge, "Troy?"

This time he came in much more clearly, "Can you make it?"

"What?"

"Caleb, it's the only way to reach your group before sundown." I looked at the meter of space in between me and the next part of ridge. I took a deep breath. "If you can't make it don't try it Caleb. It's not-"

"I can make it." I spoke to myself, ignoring Troy. I judged the space. Judging how far I would have to jump in order to make it. I checked the balance gauge on my suit. The suit's scanner read 50%, fair.

It could be better, I thought, but I can do this. I took a step and then leaped into the air. My suit immediately started blinking a red light signaling that my jump was going to be too short. I spread my legs a little farther apart and the suit's scanner blinked green just as I touched the ground with my front foot. I relaxed about to set my back foot down beside it right when a huge crack sprouted three meters in front of me.

"Don't move!" This time Troy was begging me, "Caleb, please do not move." I couldn't just stand there. My ready-for-battle body was anxious and before I knew it I had shifted my weight.

The crack grew more. It stretched across the entire ridge now. Now it was threatening to break loose.

"Caleb…" I shut Troy's voice out of my head. I heard a cracking noise and knew that I had less than a second before the rock would break away.

I touched a button on my suit. The rock broke away just as I shot a grappling hook out of my suit. I heard Troy gasp.

The hook lodged itself on the not broken rock, I hung there breathing hard, and then I slowly worked my way up the long rope that was attached. Finally, I made it to the top and I slid onto the ledge, panting.

"Good work. You only have 10 meters of ledge left and then you will hit ground. From there finding your group should be easy." Troy hesitated on the last part. The hesitation signaled to me that there was something going on. I cut Troy off from his rambling.

"Troy?" He paused. "What is in the way between me and my group?" Troy hesitated as if not sure how to respond.

"It might not happen. It's a 1 in 100 chance of happening."

"Troy, what might happen?"

"There is a slight possibility of a beast fight. The fight would occur in the spot where you must cross to get to your group. I don't know for sure if it will happen. Once you get closer I will be able to tell. If there is a fight you do not have enough time to make your way all the way around before sundown."

I looked up at the sky. The sun was a yellow ball right above the horizon. I looked at my forearm of my suit. One hour of sunlight left. Then, I started to run.

"Tell me where to go." The gravelly surface was hard to run on. Rocks slipped out from underneath my feet. I leaped onto a large rock to continue on my path.

"Okay, run northwest." I directed myself so that I was running directly for the sun. And I kept running, "You should reach your destination in about 30 minutes. You might make it before the fight." Troy sighed, "I still cannot tell if the beasts are there or not." I was breathing hard, but I urged myself to go faster. I only had 30 more minutes of running if I reached the spot in time, only 30 more minutes.

"On my charts it shows me that you are going to make it. I am still not positive though. I will keep an eye out." I kept running.

I felt minutes go by. I was still running. I was still keeping up my pace until I saw something in the distance. I could not make out what they were at first. They looked like little pinpricks of light. However, as I got closer, the way their bright red and yellow lights flickered against the setting sun gave them away. There were fires in the distance. When there were fires that meant life.

"Troy do you see what I see?"

"Yes," Troy paused, "I can't tell you who it is or what they are doing though. Get closer I may be able to get a better reading on what or who they are."

I kept running, more quietly this time. I was sneaking up on this group. I was trying to figure out what they were doing. I closed in on the spot. Hiding behind a rock, I stuck my head out, and almost fell backwards by the surprising sight that I saw.

There were people. A lot of them, tents were set up to make something sort of like a village. People ran around, some were doing work. Small children were playing. They were running around with bare feet.

Women tended to the fires. They wore clothing that I had never seen before. Most of the women wore clothes around their heads.

To me it was like what life used to be like before the Resistances were fully set up. This village looked, to me, like it had looked before we had gained civilization again. Many men stood guard around the perimeter of the village as if to defend the village from beasts and other enemies.

“What the heck?” I was confused. I didn’t know that these people were ever set up here or why.

I put my forearm up to my mouth, “Troy, what are these people doing-” Then I was cut off by a harsh sounding voice. The voice had a strange accent. I felt the hairs on the back of my neck stand up.

“Move one more muscle and you’re dead.”

CHAPTER 5

I froze, and turned around slowly to come face to face with the barrel of a gun. I looked up at the man who had spoke. The man had short hair with a shaggy beard. His eyes were a dark brown, but shone brightly in the darkness. He wore a sleeveless shirt. The man had huge muscled arms but he was shorter than me, no more than five feet nine inches tall.

"Get up." The man spoke again. "Put your hands behind your head." The sound of his voice surprised me. It was cruel and demanding and I followed his orders right away.

I moved slowly to not surprise him. First putting my hands behind my head and then standing, slowly. Once I was fully standing he nudged me with the barrel of his gun. "Turn around and walk forward."

I did as I was told walking straight into the village. As soon as I stepped in, everyone, even the children, stopped what they were doing and stared at me. They all had scared yet awed looks on their faces. It was as if this situation didn't happen often. The man who had found me kept me moving forward, the barrel of his gun nudged into the upper part of my back.

Finally, after all of the silence we reached a tent larger than the rest. The tent had a plume of smoke coming out of the top. "Go inside." The man ordered.

I leaned over and walked into the tent, closely followed by the man who had captured me. There were three men in the tent. The center one was younger than the other two. He seemed the same age as the man who had captured me. The other two on either side of him both had pipes coming out of their mouths. They looked older and more experienced. However, it was the young man who spoke.

"Trithon? Who is this? Why is he here?" The middle one spoke, he also had the same strange accent as the man who captured me. It was an accent that I had never heard before I met this group.

"Czar, this is a boy who I found outside of our village. He seemed to be snooping. I think that he is a spy from the Resistance." When he said the word Resistance he snarled as if saying the word was a sin. So these people are not fond of the Resistance, I thought. The man, Trithon, continued speaking, "We should question him. He is probably going to call into the Resistance right now."

Moving slowly I turned my suit's volume up to high so that Troy could hear everything that was said. I looked up. The Czar was looking at me with curiosity. He had a dark skin color. His hair and eyes matched, both of them dark brown.

"Trithon, relax." The Czar sat there. "What is your name boy?"

"My name is Caleb Hanson."

"Are you a spy?" He asked me, there was a sort of curiosity in his voice, "We don't get many visitors."

I debated how I should answer, choosing my words carefully. "No, I am not a spy. I am rebelling from the Resistance. Me and a group of about 30, I was the leader of my group. We were separated, now I am just trying to find them again."

"Why are you rebelling?" The Czar asked. He had surprise in his voice now.

"I think that there is something else out there, something in the fallen Resistances of China, Asia, or Russia. I want to figure out who is trying to wipe our community out, who is trying to kill us all." The Czar looked at me with a new emotion on his face, admiration.

"We have had many problems with beasts. They have wiped out more than half of our community, taking with them both children and women along with some of our best fighters. We thought that the Resistance had been sending them onto us, trying to wipe us out, that is why we are so cautious about our surroundings, about anyone that is not like us around our community."

"Why are you not with the Resistance, why are you against them?" I asked. I was the one curious now. I did not like the Resistance but I doubted that it was for the same reason as these people. The Czar frowned, as if lost in memory.

"A long time ago, before the radiation, my people were part of a country. This country was called Russia. Our land was not connected to your land. There was an ocean in between here and North America. When the radiation hit many of our people were wiped out, but some of us survived. Years after the radiation hit the plates below us shifted, moving the large continents so that they were all connected just like they were a very long time ago. We have now learned that we only survived because our immune systems were strong enough to fight the radiation right out of our bodies. Most of us were living in huts like this village that we have set up. We were great fighters. Russia was one of the best Resistances that had been set up. We had top fighters and the best doctors. We also had the top researchers and scientists. We were finding bugs, keeping track of their progress. We learned by our research something that you believe, that there is something else out there, something else is controlling them. Just as we figured this out, a pack hit.

"Millions of beasts raided our Resistance. They killed most of our people, most of our fighters, and most of our scientists. We went to the North American Resistance asking for help. We, the dominant Russians asking North America for help," The Czar chuckled under his breath. "Oh, but the North American Resistance wanted to be world known too. They wanted to be the best, better than the Russians.

"So they denied us access to their Resistance. They said that they were not going to let us in. They turned us away, wanting to have all of the glory by themselves. They still think that they can save the world by themselves, with only one Resistance left. They think that they can hold the beasts off. They think that there still is hope. They are wrong.

"Right now, whoever is controlling the beasts is gathering them up, preparing for the final pounce, the last one that will completely wipe out mankind. Whoever and whatever is controlling the beasts is smart. They took out many of the Resistances of great power first, ending with North America. They want this grand finale." The Czar shook his head back and forth, then. "We have offered our help many times before, each time your general has turned us down, not accepting our help. He has no idea what he has gotten himself into. Humanity will fall. The era of the creatures will begin." The Czar looked at me. I sat there in a daze. I had gotten a lot of information all at once, and had just started to process it.

"The other day another break-in happened. I don't think that anyone was killed, not many were injured either, it was much unlike the last time."

"Hmm, so the officers took care of it?"

"No," the Czar looked at me with surprise, before I continued "I did." I said firmly. "My brother Justin and I took it down."

"I have never heard of a boy taking a beast down." The Czar looked at me intently. He paused and looked at the men on either side of him, then at Trithon. Finally, he looked back at me. I was ready for the catch, ready for what would happen to me now. Suddenly, the Czar spoke. "Before we decide what to do with you, I want to see if you are as good as you say that you are."

I was in a pit. There were five people facing me down, they all carried wooden sticks and were all older than me, about 20 to 25. The night was brisk, only a few stars shone down but the moon was out and bright casting a glow into the pit. I was holding a wooden stick as well, facing down my attackers. This was my tenth fight of the night. The Czar had started me easy, working me up until I was battling the top fighters, and then more than one at a time.

Now the Russian fighters thought that they had me, they thought that they could take me down with five. I breathed in through my nose and then back out through my mouth. I felt the cold night air, the pressure and weight of it, I felt the ground under my feet, soft and fragile yet stable. I looked into my attackers eyes. They were so deep, so dark, they wanted to beat me. As if I was listening through earmuffs I heard the cheering, the stands were full. Everyone wanted to see this new person fight for his way out. The fight started.

Two of the attackers went forward, surrounding me. I could tell that this group had fought together before, that they knew what they were doing. The other three stayed in front of me. The front guy that was in the middle was Trithon. He had a grim expression on his face. I could tell that he had wanted to take me alone. I could tell that he wanted his shot.

Then, Trithon said something in Russian that I could not make out. He charged forward, his stick was raised above his head.

One of his teammates yelled, "Нет!" It sounded like a warning. Trithon seemed to ignore the warning and continue onward.

I saw my chance, I jumped into the air, and kicked forward, my foot connected easily with Trithon's gut. He crumpled to the ground as I landed gracefully by his side. The rest of Trithon's team continued circling me. They all had scared expressions on their faces. The man who shouted at Trithon spoke again in Russian, this time I could tell that it was some sort of counting.

On the last word that he said, all four fighters charged at me, one of them reached me first, swinging his wooden stick around, trying to hit my head, I ducked underneath and swung my legs out in front of me, connecting with his shins. He fell to the ground in pain, clutching his shins to his body.

Two of them reached me at once. One took my left side and the other one took my right side. Both of them swung at my sides at the same time, I dodged one and parried the other. Then, I changed my momentum and direction to jab one of them in the gut. Next, I swung my stick around to smack the other Russian in the back. Both of the men fell to the ground in pain.

The last one stood six meters away. He was eyeing me up, watching my fighting technique. He then thrust his sword past his arm into his side taking up a martial arts position. I vaguely remembered when I was seven or eight years old, taking my school class of martial arts. My teacher was walking by me, checking everyone's positions. I had taken up my own stance, mine was unique much different from any of the others. My stick was raised above my head, my arm out in a protective position.

I came back into the moment. The man was still facing me in his martial arts stance. I got into my own, putting my hand out, urging him to come at me. He did, he sprinted at me and swung his stick at my head, I parried, and from there we got into a battle. He was good. His stick moved about me fast, I was fast too, blocking all of his blows, waiting for the right moment to attack.

I kicked my leg out and he deflected, I saw where he was going to hit next and parried his blow to my ankle. I was gaining on him, on the attack mode. But then he lashed out and hit my side. I crumpled and he saw his chance, he started gaining on me, I was just barely parrying the blows backing up slowly. I was slowly and steadily losing my lead and ground.

We were fast, the series of blows came rapidly, hit, hit, hit, and hit. I was surprised by how good his endurance was. He was a great fighter. Slowly I was losing confidence, realizing that this man might actually beat me.

"Fear means failure. It is a choice, an element of something that might happen. You can choose not to fear and when you accomplish this, you will be unstoppable." My father's words came back to me, so smoothly. I remembered his voice so easily. I could hear it inside of my head. I knew what he would do if he was in this situation. "You will learn not to fear." *Not to fear, not to fear.* I could do this.

That's when my situation changed. I saw the Russian man's moves, how he moved, his rhythm, his technique. I saw how he battled me. Saw his strengths and his weaknesses. Blow, feint left, blow right, feint right, hit left, blow down the middle, feint left…

This method repeated over and over. Finally, I saw my chance, after his blow, I knew that he was going to feint left, so I lunged forward, just as he did his feint left, I jabbed him hard in the rib cage. By doing this I heard a breath of air come out in a huff. Now I knew that I had the advantage, I kept attacking. Lunging forward at him, I swung my stick hard, smacking him hard across the stomach. Finally he fell.

I stood there in the cold night, not thinking, not moving. Finally, I felt a hand on my shoulder. I turned startled, then I saw a familiar face, he was looking at me with admiration, and a hint of jealousy.

"Trithon," I breathed.

"Man, you just won." He spoke happily. He was congratulating me. I felt my hand move up to my head and run through my hair. Trithon smiled and chuckled at my gesture, his eyes were bright. "You have proven to the Czar your powers, now he will determine how to assess and what to do with you."

"What will he do with me?" I asked puzzlement on my features. Trithon's face fell when I asked, his eyes turned sad. "Well, what do you usually do when people walk into your village?"

"We kill them." Trithon's voice was flat as if he truly did not want to tell me that. My heart dropped. After all this, chances of life and death, the Czar was going to kill me? I felt like sitting down on the ground, curling up into a ball and crying, crying for my father, for Justin, for this mission.

"Right this way." A man that I had never seen before was standing in front of me. He was probably around Trithon's age. I looked behind me, Trithon was no longer there. Instead he was replaced by another man that I had never seen before. To my right and left were also people that I didn't know. I thought of taking them out, I could do it. Then I realized that would be a form of retaliation and a sign for the Czar.

Instead, I followed the man who had spoken. We walked around the side of the village to the west-facing side, furthest from the Resistance. Behind the hut was a group of people, no more than 15 of them. They all stood with bags over their shoulders. In the center was a man that I had seen before, the Czar. Finally we reached the group. The Czar spoke, "Caleb Hanson, you are a great fighter.

"I have put together a group of my top fighters. They will accompany you on your journey. All of them wanted to join you, you are their commander now." The Czar handed me a bag, "In here is food, water, and tools, and weapons that you might need on your journey." I scanned the faces of the men in my group, yes. There he was, in the center of the group, Trithon.

"Thank you, Czar, I appreciate this very much." The Czar smiled, and then he spoke for the last time.

"Now go out there and save the world."

I turned, shouldered my bag and took off into the night, hoping that my new recruits were following me. After a pause I heard heavy footsteps, slowly turning to a run, following me. For the first time since I had gotten my new group I felt a feeling of accomplishment. I turned to my forearm.

"Troy, I am out of that encampment, I am traveling west, toward the region of California. Copy back when you hear this message."

I ran off into the night.

CHAPTER 6

"Troy? Are you there? I repeat, Troy, do you copy?" I threw down my long distance receiver in disgust. Then I turned to my new group. They were close together, huddled to keep warm in the cold evening. The sun had just set behind the horizon giving our surrounding a dark feel. I was guessing that we were somewhere near the Nevada region.

Everyone in my group clutched their steaming hot noodles in small bowls close to their bodies to keep staying warm. My suit told me that the temperature was 42 degrees. I silently thanked Troy for packing me the portage food maker. My suit had closed around me protectively making it seem like I was in winter gear. Most of the Russians weren't as fortunate as me. Many of them were dressed in clothes that were meant for fighting so they were loose and dangled from their backs.

It had been three days now that Troy hadn't contacted me, I was worrying, both for my group and Troy.

"Once you guys are done with your dinner you should try to get to sleep. We are leaving at sunrise tomorrow." Many of the men grumbled. But they still turned over onto their backs or sides to sleep. We've done nothing but travel for days. Nothing had come after us. No beast nor bug nor even people from the Resistance. Something was sure to find us soon. I sat there for a while, letting the cool night air surround me, I had no idea that it was going to be this hard to find my group. I also had no idea that I was going to be joined by people that I barely knew. Something is bound to go wrong, I thought, something is going to happen soon. I saw movement out of the corner of my eye. I turned and saw Trithon walking over to me.

"How do you do it?" He asked.

"Do what?"

"Stay strong for us, I can tell that something is bugging you." His brown eyes looked into mine thoughtfully. I sighed.

"I just want to get back to my group. I have no idea where they are or what challenges they are facing. For all I know they might be fighting a beast now. I don't even know if we are going in the right direction."

Trithon nodded, "Every good leader is going to face something that is bugging them, and every good leader will face it head on and succeed in accomplishing the task." Trithon paused, "Hanson, you are a good leader, I have no idea how you do it, I don't know what is going on in your life, all I know is that I will follow you anywhere and believe in what you say and do." I smiled in the cold night. Trithon continued, "It's been quiet for a while, I mean, we haven't faced any beasts for a long time."

"I know. I've been getting vague feelings as if I am being watched." I yawned.

"You better get some shut eye. We are going to have to wake up early tomorrow. I'll take first watch." Trithon nodded at me, "Really, go and sleep," he insisted. I reluctantly agreed. It had been a long time since I had gotten a full night's sleep. I lay down on the hard, cold ground and closed my eyes. I did not think that I would sleep but I felt myself drift off. I soon fell into a deep sleep.

I was in a room. My father was sitting in a metal chair in the middle of the room, his head was hung down so that it was resting hard on his chest, and his eyes were closed. There were no windows in the room and only one door. I heard the door open and turned to see who had entered, it looked like a human, walking on two legs, with arms swinging by his side, and he had two eyes and a mouth, just like a human.

There was some part of me telling me that this was not a human, but his features looked so human, almost too human. He was walking to the center of the room, towards the place where my dad was sitting.

Then I saw it, it was something in the way that the strange man moved, too fast, too choppy. Then I saw that my dad's arms were strapped behind the chair. The strange man stooped in front of the chair, kneeling down in front of my father. He made my father look at him, but my father did not open his eyes. I had a feeling in my stomach that if my father didn't open his eyes something very bad was going to happen to him.

"Dad open your eyes, dad please." I pleaded softly. My father's eyes shot open, they were an ultraviolet green, as if they were robotic. They shifted back and forth ever so slightly. Then they found me. He stared at me with intensity, as if his eyes were going to burn a hole in my soul.

"Dad no," I cried out, "Please, no!"

A hand touched my shoulder and I immediately grabbed the arm and threw the man who had touched my shoulder to the ground.

My eyes shot open and I bolted up to my feet. I looked at my surroundings, something had touched my shoulder. Looking around I saw nothing. Then I looked down. There, Trithon lay, clutching his arm, I kneeled down.

"Caleb," Trithon sputtered, "they're here." Right as Trithon said that millions of red eyes shot out of the dark night, the eyes were no more than my chest height, but they surrounded my group.

"Attention!" I yelled into the night. Bodies around me started flailing around. Behind me around 15 men stood. We were ready to take these red eyed beasts down.

From my back I pulled out a fire starter and threw in on the ground in front of me. It sprouted up in flames right as it touched the ground, illuminating the beasts. My suit blinked red, part leopard-part wolf, one of the most dangerous beasts known. These beasts travel in packs. They were closing in on us. I knew that all of their minds were in sync, ready to attack whenever the moment occurred.

"Men, hold your ground!" There were at least 50 eyes, gleaming at us from the dark. They were stalking us. They were waiting until our hold on the ground faltered.

I heard a howling sound, the beasts had started howling. I could hear the breathing of my group. They were all wide awake now. The cold night pressed down on us, I could feel the coldness and the sweat, and most of all I could smell the fear, and taste it in the air. I was sure that the beasts could too.

The beast in front of me stepped forward, so did the rest of the pack, "Hold your ground!" I yelled over the loud howling. "We can take them!" I felt a man's presence beside me. I looked to the side and saw Trithon standing there. He looked into my eyes.

"I have your back," he said softly, so that only I could hear him. He held a spear in his hands, "Let's do this." His expression was so confident I believed him. I turned my attention back to the beast in front of me. It was about three meters away I could see the saliva dripping from its teeth, it was growling loudly. I could tell that it was hungry and wanted to take me down.

It leaped at me, its claws were held out in front of him. The beast wanted to catch me and hold me down. I swung my cutlass around and sliced the beast in the stomach, it fell to the ground just as the other surrounding beasts jumped at us from all sides.

We were ready, some of us fell but others fought through waiting until the next wave attacked and pulling injured behind them, out of harm's way. I fought through the beasts in front of me, feeling Trithon's presence by my side. He was strong and so was I.

Together we made our way through the sea of beasts. I realized why I liked Trithon's presence so much. It reminded me of Justin, Justin…

I was momentarily distracted from the fight and a beast leaped into the air, I dodged, then turned and stabbed it with my cutlass.

What I realized was that there was a lot more than just 50 beasts, the howling had probably summoned more beasts to the mix. Two beasts jumped at me and with my cutlass I sliced them down, I looked around, our group of 15 had gone down to no more than 10. We needed to get rid of these beasts soon. I saw another man drop.

I turned back around, this time at least 10 beasts were looking at me, growling and showing their arm-long fangs. They wanted to take me down, as a pack. They all attacked me at once.

Their minds were so attuned to each other that they worked in unison. Unison was the hardest to defeat.

Two leaped into the air, one going for my left shoulder, the other going for my right shoulder. With my cutlass I was able to fend them off. Both of them fell to the ground, dead. Just as I recovered one jumped for my back and grabbed at my shoulder blades, I felt the claws sink into my flesh. I yelled in pain and stabbed my cutlass backward, getting it off of me. I could feel the blood dripping down my back as the other beasts started circling me again. There were still a lot left.

I grabbed my knives from two side sheaths of my suit. I threw the one in my left hand hard at the wolf leopard closest to me. The knife lodged into its chest and the beast sank to the ground. Then, feeling the presence of a beast behind me I turned and threw the knife in my right hand backwards. It went right pasted Trithon's left ear and nailed the beast that was getting ready to jump on him in the side. Trithon looked at me. A silent thanks appeared on his features.

I turned back to the beasts that had been circling me, they were backing up, back into the night, all of them were whimpering. Finally they disappeared into the dark black.

I looked behind me at the men who were still standing. There were only about seven people up. The rest of them were on the ground, rolling around in pain. One man did not look much older than my age of 17. He looked like he was only a boy. He was leaning over a man who wasn't moving.

"Survey?" I asked him. The boy looked up at me, there were tears brimming in his eyes. I crouched down beside him.

"I- I think that he's... dead," The tears started running down the boy's cheeks. He looked no more than 19. The man lying on the ground looked like he could be this boy's brother. I leaned over the man lying on the ground and put my first two fingers on the man's neck. I could feel a vague pulse.

"Does he have any cuts or claw marks?" I asked the 19 year old that was beside me.

"No." The boy had regained control but he was breathing hard.

"Don't worry," I smiled at the boy, "your brother is alive. He will wake up shortly. When he does wake up, come and get me."

With that I stood, patted the boy on the back and made my way to the next injury. Looking at the bodies laying on the ground I knew that it was going to be a long night.

"It has now been a week since Troy has contacted me, I am glad that I have the portage so that my group does not go hungry but I am still unsure if we are traveling the right path. A couple nights ago we were attacked by wolf leopards, we had no deaths but many injuries, we are now moving at an even slower pace than before. I am guessing that we are nearing the end of the California region, about to reach New Russia.

"From there we will follow the plan and travel toward the China province. Please contact when you have heard this message." I let my wrist drop slowly to my side and took a deep breath, I could do this without Troy, and I had to now.

I had no idea where he was, or why he wasn't responding, I could only hope that I had been in a dark spot so that he was there and I just couldn't hear him.

I looked out over my group, it was still cold, my group huddled together, protecting the injured and trying to stay warm. My cheeks felt flushed and I could feel the brisk air on my face. I took another deep breath, letting my thoughts come and go. This mission had not gone at all as planned. I had lost my group early on and had not managed to catch up with them.

"Men, we are going to be reaching the New Russia region shortly. This region is probably less than 14 hours away. Once we get there we will be hit with a major hot spell. Be ready."

One man spoke up. "How will we find the creators of the beasts?" I nodded at his question.

"Once we reach New Russia we will change our route to northward and make our way toward the Old China Resistance. If my predictions are correct the creators should be in the heart of that territory." The man nodded, as if my words had made total sense to him, they went back to what they had been doing before, talking, eating, and just trying to stay warm and get their minds off of the situation.

Now, after all that I had been through I was beginning to

doubt this mission myself, my grandfather's words came back to me, so sharp and crisp in my mind. *This mission cannot fail. This is a category 10 mission. In this mission you will save the world.*

I could still hear the tone of his voice, he was a commanding officer at heart and any soldier would be willing to follow him into battle. Then I remembered my father's words, the words that I could never forget, the words that had stayed with me all this time, *do not let go.*

I was that little kid again, no more than 6 years old. I was going to my first martial arts training. I was dressed in white martial arts clothing, my light blonde hair shone in the light of the day. I was holding my stick, the first one that I had ever held. It was as tall as me but felt right in my hand. I was proud of myself. Now I could see it in the way I stood. I wanted my father to be proud of me too. He looked at me, a soft smile was on his face but it didn't reach his eyes. I looked up and saw my grandfather's face above mine.

He was smiling, ever so proud. I looked back at my father his smile had gone away and it was now replaced by a frown.

I wanted to scream at him, 'Why can't you be proud of me? I will be just as good as you one day! Please, daddy, please be proud of me. What is it that you want from me? Can't you just be proud, for once?'

Then my grandfather's words came back *he would be proud if he saw you now.* He would be proud. I am a leader. I can complete this mission and find my group again. I can do this.

I opened my eyes. Everyone in the Russian group was asleep except for two watch people. I stood and they looked up, "I'll be back soon." They nodded and I took off into the night. There was somewhere that I needed to be, something told me that I had to be there, and soon.

I looked into the sky and saw a hill, not a very large one but it stretched out in front of me. I took off up the hill running at full speed. Finally, I reached the top. Once I got there I paused for a moment and turned. I looked back at where we had just come. I looked out at the plain below. Suddenly, I started hearing a strange sound. It was the sound of feet thumping in a rhythmic pattern. I turned again and looked down the other side of the hill. What I saw made me take a big breath in surprise.

The group looked like an army, sent out for one purpose, to kill. The army stretched out over into the horizon, it was huge, I saw beasts, thousands of them, many different types, and I saw bugs and different creatures too. There weren't as many of these strange creatures but there didn't have to be, just by looking at them, all of my courage from before was drained of me, as if they were a negative energy source.

They looked like humans. They had all the same features as humans. These creatures even walked on two legs. But there was something strange, something different about them, about the way that they moved. They moved awkwardly, as if they shouldn't have to obey the laws of gravity. They moved fast too. Their walk was quick. Their legs moved very effortlessly through the night.

I could feel myself tense. I wanted to take all of these strange new creatures out right away, right now. I could feel my body want to take off. I could feel myself want to start traveling down the hill.

I felt two firm hands grasp my back and shove me to the ground. The shove was hard. I fell down just as the strange creature closest to us turned its head, looking in my direction. Somehow this person had known that a creature would look.

"Don't move," the voice whispered softly in my ear. The voice was so familiar, but I couldn't place it, "Stay where you are." Finally, the creature turned its head back around and kept moving with the army. The hand pressing down on my back slowly released its strong hold. I turned and came face to face with big, dark, brown eyes and brown hair.

"Justin?" I asked. Shock was etched across my face. I was so confused that I barely processed what was going on. Justin smiled, his teeth shone bright in the moonlight. "Justin!" I exclaimed. I grabbed him and pulled him into huge hug. Then I realized what just happened. I realized that somehow Justin had found me. I also realized that the group was nowhere to be seen. "Wait, what happened? Why aren't you with the group?" Justin's smile dropped quickly to a frown.

"I lost them," Justin mumbled out fast.

"You, what, lost them?" I was angry at first, and then just confused, "wait, what happened?"

Justin took a deep breath and then started his story. "After a couple days, I thought that the group was doing fine, so I tried to come after you, I wanted to know that you were okay and the communication services weren't working properly. I needed to help you. I sent Jones and the group onward and promised to meet them at the crossing point between the North American Resistance and the New Russian one, so I went after you, trying to retrace your steps. I came across a strange group of Russians and thought they might have killed you, I talked to their leader and he told me that he had sent you on your way. I kept up on your path and came across a bunch of dead wolf leopards. I heard wolves howling so I took off from there. Then, I heard an army, I came up this hill and saw you standing there, you looked like you were going to march down there so I went and tackled you." Justin looked at me and smiled.

"The communication didn't work for you either?"

"No," Justin shook his head, serious again. Then his eyes got huge as if he realized something. "Wait, does that mean that there is something wrong with Troy?"

"I hope not," I looked down at my arm band on my suit. Just then I heard a noise that was filled with static. Voices started speaking.

"Caleb Hanson, this is your general speaking. I know what you are trying to do and I can assure you that it will not work. I have captured Troy so you have no more home base options." The general laughed a little with that sentence. "You are on your own out there. I am sending a squad of officials out there after you, and I promise, they will find you, and when they do there will be no more of you. This is the last time that you will embarrass me in front of the entire Resistance."

The general paused, "You will not come close at all to reaching your goal of 'saving the world' because in my eyes, it is already saved." The general laughed, "the world is in my hands now, Caleb, and if you come back… Well, let's just say that won't happen."

I looked down at the marching army. Most of them were gone now, only a few were left. They were probably off to defeat our Resistance, the last standing Resistance. They were probably marching to the general's front door right now.

The general had no idea what was in store for him. I could

feel the cold night air on my face, I could hear the sound of the beasts howling in the night, and then I did not hear anything, the night was still. I put my forearm up to my mouth ready to speak back to the general.

Justin's hand pushed it away, "If you speak into the receiver he will know where we are and it will be even easier for him to come after us." Justin was so sure of what he said, he was sure that he was going with me, us.

I paused and touched the red button on my suit, the one that turns off the receiver mode. Then I let my arm drop back down at my side. I felt empty now, as if everything that I had ever dreamed of happening was suddenly ripped away from me, and thrown into an abyss.

I fell to the ground. I felt the weight of what was happening press down on me for the first time of the whole mission. It felt like I was bearing the weight all on my shoulders, making me crumple. I just wanted to be home, with my dad, with Justin and with grandfather. I wanted none of this to have ever happened to me.

I was on the brink of death. It was facing me on all sides, looking down at me, ready to pounce when my guard was down. I felt my body start to shut down, the weight of what was happening and the stress was too much. I set my head in my hands. Success seemed to be a lost cause now.

That's when Justin sat down beside me. He took a deep breath and let it out slowly. Then he did it again, on the third time I joined him, copying his technique and breathing in and out, in and out. We sat there for a while, until he spoke.

"Remember when we were young and we were running through the halls of the Martial Arts Center?" He smiled at the memory. I looked at him, "You always wanted to impress me as my little brother, you always wanted to be better than me, and now you are."

Justin paused and glanced at me, I didn't respond, "This time you wanted to show me how fast you could run so you took off, I didn't want to be beat by my five year old brother so I took off too.

"We were sprinting through the hallways, our little legs were pumping so fast and hard, we weren't even paying attention to where we were going and we smashed right into Mrs. Cardel. We both fell to the ground hard. Remember how we each got red cards from our teachers for running through the halls and we had to do 12 hours of service work each. That was a lot for little kids."

I was laughing now, so caught up in Justin's story that I had momentarily forgotten what we still had to do.

I kept laughing. I just couldn't stop. It seemed like all of that weight that had been pressing down just seemed to wash away with the laughter. Justin continued talking, "After that, we were inseparable, but I still always wanted to beat you in everything that we did.

"Remember when we were doing our first actual battles, one vs. one?" I nodded, "you were taking everyone down, but I thought that I could beat you, I went up to the teacher and challenged you. The teacher let us fight.

"I remember…" he laughed softly to himself, "I went in hard, raising my stick over my head and making a war cry, all you had to do we swing your stick horizontal and I was down, I was so embarrassed." I nodded again, laughing so hard at the memory that my abs hurt. Justin started laughing again too.

I just wanted to stay in that period of time, just be there again with Justin. Just be able to be a kid again. Now, I had so much expectation ahead of me. *People expect great things from you, Caleb.*

My father's words were played inside my head, like so many times before. *You just keep showing people what you are capable of doing.* I can do it, I've come this far and I am prepared for the worst, I stood, stretching my tired legs.

"Let's do this." I heard the confidence in my voice, Justin stood up with me, he was taller and older than me but I knew that he would follow any of my commands.

"Come with me." I turned and made my way down the hill, away from that one moment of childhood memory, away from that moment of being a kid. I made my way back towards my life, back towards the pain and grit of it all, back towards saving the world. But this time, I was prepared. I was ready for what was coming for me.

I was ready for everything and anything now.

CHAPTER 7

There was something up ahead of us. In the dark night I couldn't tell what it was but I could sense something was there. I held up my hand and, sensing my movement, everyone behind me stopped moving. I gave the signal to take out weapons and heard my group shuffling around behind me. I grasped the smooth surface of my cutlass tightly. Though it was smooth it was also full of grip.

I heard Justin pull back his bowstring, notching an arrow. I edged my way forward, careful not to make much noise. Up ahead something black stood out in the already black night, something darker. Finally I reached it, I put my hand on its smooth surface and felt a bumpy like texture, it was cold, colder than anything I had felt before, I pulled my hand away immediately, then I pushed my left forearm to the surface.

"Analyze," I whispered softly into the cool night. My suit beeped and I pulled it away. Rock, the suit read.

Slowly I felt my way around the rock, keeping my fingertips pressing softly against the cool surface. The rock went on for a long time. I felt its smooth and cold surface, brushing up, it was there always there, smooth and cold. Then, a drop, my fingers pressed into a space in between a crack in the rock. I kept walking and the rock went back up again to the same, smooth surface as before. I retraced my steps and went back to that crack in the rock.

My fingers felt around in that crack, prying trying to see if there was any leverage. Then, my fingers traveled downwards, the crack continued, in a straight line, my hand went all the way down until it touched the ground and the crack widened.

Then I traced the crack back up as far as I could reach, the crack stopped, but then my fingers felt something more. They started traveling to the left, and the crack continued for a meter and then stopped again. This time my hand traveled downward, outlining the frame of a door. I stepped back, confused. Why was a door in a rock?

Justin came up to my side.

"It's a door," I breathed softly.

"Open it." I looked at Justin, "well if it's a door, it should open."

I stepped back to the rock, and my fingers grasped the ridge again. This time, I pushed forward, there was some movement but the door was much too heavy. Justin came up by my side and he pushed too. Together we pushed the rock out of our way and stepped into a dark hallway. The door closed immediately behind us, and a lantern blazed to life on our left. I gripped my cutlass tighter and started walking forward, very slowly.

There was a musty smell in the hallway, like mold, and the hallway had a very Earthy feel to it. The ground was hard, made up of dirt, as if whoever had paved this hallway had not cared what it looked like.

The walls were pure stone, not smooth, they looked like they had been cut hastily as if whoever had made this rock tunnel had wanted it fast. There was a bend in the path that Justin and I followed. Just as we turned the corner a light on my suit started blinking red, the air quality in here was very poor, 5 minutes of breathing left.

I removed my mask from my back and placed it over my mouth and nose, breathing in the cool pure oxygen. I could hear Justin's breathing too, loud now, in his mask. My eyes scanned the hallway ahead of us, up ahead was another lantern. I looked up and around at the walls around us.

They were just as bare as the walls before but there was something else among them, something that I couldn't grasp, but something more. I started walking again, we continued down the hallway. I was getting more and more curious. Something was bugging me, nagging me in the back of my mind. I ignored it and kept moving, ever so quietly towards a small light that had appeared at the end of the tunnel.

I was anxious now, my body craved for something to be found out, yet I held myself back, making myself go slowly through the hallways. Finally we reached the end of the tunnel. There was a small entry way, some sort of doorway.

Quietly, I stepped inside, feeling moist air on my face. We were in a room sort of like a chamber. There was a wall between us and the rest of the room. I walked around it, being careful not to make noise.

Then I heard noises that I definitely wasn't expecting, voices. I peered around the side of the wall quietly, careful not to be seen. What I saw surprised me even more, people, at least 30 of them, all of them were sitting around a large table. There was some sort of blueprint in the middle, a battle plan.

One man was standing up pointing to sections of the blueprint and describing, step by step, what was going to happen. His hand moved, and I saw something different, something that a human wouldn't be capable of doing, something faster.

His hand. Then I realized, these people weren't humans, they were some sort of creature, the creature. I thought back to my conversation with my grandfather.

"My guess is that whoever is controlling the animals has finally figured out where we are training our children. Now they are going to keep attacking our community more and more because now they know our weakness."

There is a higher power, something or someone, controlling the beasts and controlling the bugs. That is what these creatures are. Trying to control human life, and put an end to it. Some creature like the one's in the other room. Some creature that killed my father, some creature that will do whatever they can to destroy me and humankind, some creature that I could take out right now.

Justin must have seen my body tense, because immediately I felt a hand on my shoulder, soft yet strong. My body relaxed, the man-creature was still talking, his hands were moving fast, much faster than a human's. I didn't know how I saw the resemblance of him and a human in the first place.

The creature moved in on the blueprint and it enlarged on a

spot, the last standing Resistance, North America. Then the creature zoomed in on another spot in the high altitudes of China, the first fallen Resistance.

The creature zoomed in more. There was a building, a large, large building that took up most of the high China territory. There was an army, millions of creatures like the ones that were in front of me now. They were marching, practicing. Preparing for the final battle, on the blueprint it read, The Battle of North America.

The last battle before these creatures took control of the world, my world. I started hearing some of what the creature was saying.

"... We have an army. The humans will not be prepared. There are millions of us that will march towards their borders, accompanied by millions of beasts and bugs marching from our headquarters in China…" I was breathing heavy, "... the march will begin in about 35 days time. That is only five weeks to prepare. As the leaders you must all prepare your squads. Once we get rid of this greedy species there will be nothing in our way.

"We will be able to live life again as we know how live it, the era of the homo sapiens or "wise man" will have ended, a new era of the homo celeritas or "fast man" will have been started!"

With those words the creature stepped back and all of the other creatures in the room started cheering, a cold sensation ran down my spine. We needed to leave, now. I turned to tell Justin, "We have to get-"

"You're not going anywhere," a cold voice sent shivers down my spine. I turned slowly, "you're coming with me, or I'm going to kill you friend in one blow." The man was like the creatures inside of that meeting room.

He held Justin with one arm, showing just how strong he was, with the other he held a knife and was pressing it gently against Justin's throat. I raised my cutlass, I could take him, "Better not do that if I were you," the man pressed his knife harder against Justin's throat, a drop of blood came out, I could see the fear in Justin's eyes.

Fear like I had never seen on him before. His eyes were darting around and his eyes, his brown eyes shone with such fear that it was almost contagious. "Drop your weapon," the creature ordered, I hesitated. There was such fear on Justin's face, "Drop your weapon!" The man yelled, I bent down and set my weapon on the ground. I heard another man's voice.

"What is going-" he must have seen me standing there with no weapon, and the other creature holding onto Justin. I felt a strong hand grab my arms and lurch then behind my back. I felt waves of pain crash through my shoulders, then a wave of despair. We were so close. I was so close. The man dragged me into the room and the meeting stopped. The lead creature spoke.

"What do we have here?" There was surprise in his voice.

"Eavesdroppers," the creature that had found us out answered. Anger towards him washed through me. "My guess is that they are from the Resistance."

The lead creature frowned. "Put them in the trucks, we will take them with us to China, from there we will let the general do what he wants with them." I felt the creature that was holding my arms with such strength, nod, then he shoved me forward, almost making me fall. I stumbled.

"Move," the creature's gruff voice held no emotion. He grabbed my arms harder and I gasped in pain. "I said move."

The creature led me out a door through the back, once we stepped outside I felt the warm and hot air on my face, we had stepped into the region of Russia, the change in temperature was so different that I faltered, surprised.

The moon had reached the top of the sky and was at its peak. It was starting its descent towards the horizon. The creature walked fast, pushing me along. He stopped at a vehicle that resembled an army truck. The only difference was that it didn't have wheels. For a moment I wondered how it moved until the creature that was holding onto me stopped moving for a moment. I felt his grip relaxed momentarily and I saw my chance.

My shoulder muscles tightened together, I could feel the strength in there. Then I forced my hands apart, the man gasped in surprise.

I changed the grip so that I was holding onto the creature instead of him holding onto me. Then, I swung my arms around my body and threw the creature over my head.

He hit the ground with a thud, I could hear the breath knocked out of him and he lay there, still. I knew that I didn't have much time until he was back on his feet. I had no idea how strong their body systems were. I also had no idea when the rest of the creatures were going to come out of the rock complex.

I turned and raced to the other truck where the creature that had been holding Justin was starting to lock up the truck. I grabbed hold of his shoulders and thrust my knee up into his back, I heard it pop and then I turned him around and thrust my knee into his stomach, the air was knocked out of him as well and he crumpled to the ground.

I grabbed the lock, it was a key lock, reaching into my suit I grabbed a tool that Troy had created to open locks and I started to dig into the lock, I heard a click and finally the lock popped open. Grabbing the door I tried to open it but it didn't open, it was stuck. I looked up and saw a retina scanner, grabbing the man that I had just taken down I opened one of his eyes and thrust it into the scanner, then, I heard another click and the door opened. I hopped inside of the truck. Justin was lying on the floor of the truck. His eyes were wide open, staring blankly at the ceiling. I grabbed his shoulders.

"Justin," I cried out, "Justin, no." I felt for my pack underneath my cutlass holder. I grabbed the medical kit, and threw it on the trucks ground at my feet. I then grabbed Justin's head and lifted it into my lap. Then I pressed my first two fingers into Justin's neck.

"Come on" I whimpered, "Please…" there was no pulse. All I could hear was the sound of my own blood in my ears, racing. I looked at my medical kit. There was a needle. I grabbed it, reading the label. *Use when heart has stopped for less than a minute, inject in neck.* Acting fast, I tore off the wrapper and held the needle lightly in my right hand.

I rested the needle on Justin's neck, then without another moment of waiting I plunged it into Justin's neck. I pulled it out slowly. Nothing. There was nothing.

"Justin?" I felt tears start to brim in my eyes. "Please, Justin, please." There was no response, I looked into Justin's dark brown eyes, they were wide open, staring at the truck's ceiling, but not seeing anything, just staring blankly.

His brown hair was resting against his forehead. His mouth was open, just a little. "Justin," I put my head to his chest, it was still warm, but I could tell that it was losing its heat. That's when I started to cry, I just let the tears come. They ran hot down my cheeks. "Justin." I clutched his hair tightly, never wanting to let go. I was never going to let go, not of Justin, not of father. I gripped his hair harder.

My cheek was resting softly against Justin's chest, I could feel my own heart racing, pumping blood, I felt the salty tears run down my cheeks, pooling up on Justin's suit. My blood was racing hard, I wasn't going to let go, never. I looked at my knuckles which were turning white from gripping Justin's hair so tightly. My tears were coming harder now.

Justin, he was standing in front of me, his hand was outstretched towards me. Then I realized, I was lying on the ground, my back was resting against the bumpy surface. Justin was offering me his hand, asking me to get up. His expression was one of concern. I reached out to take his hand.

I gripped his hand firmly and he pulled me to my feet. That's when I felt it, the pain. The pain was taking place somewhere below my knees, I tried to walk but the pain just increased. It was shooting, pain like I had never felt before, I stumbled but Justin was there. His hand shot out and he caught me, just before I hit the ground. I looked down at my knees, but all I saw was red, blood.

I looked into Justin's face, he had an expression of concern but it was also of strength and I immediately felt at peace by his expression. Then I remembered the scene that had taken place before then. A group of boys.

One lead guy, he was calling me some sort of name. Then he shoved me, hard. One of his big friends shoved me right back at him and the kid punched me across the face. I remembered falling to the ground, my knees hit first before my hands could stop me, the kid went up and kicked me in the stomach, I was on the ground.

My breath had been taken away from me. Then I remembered looking up, into Justin's face, kind and knowing. His hand was outstretched towards me ready to- thud, thud… thud, thud…

I opened my eyes. My head was resting softly against Justin's chest, there was a pool of water where my head was resting, but I didn't move my head from its spot on Justin's chest. I would not move until I believed what I heard. Then, there it was again, thud, thud… thud, thud… I started feeling my head moving in a rising and falling motion. I got up fast. Looking into Justin's face, his eyes were still open, but I could see life in them, they weren't staring blankly anymore. His mouth sputtered open and he started coughing. Just for a little, then he stopped, he looked at me and smiled.

"Well that sucked." Justin's voice came out in a croak. I smiled not knowing what to say. "What'd you go crying over me for? I appreciate the concern but couldn't you have had your memorial somewhere else? A little bit cleaner, perhaps?" Justin smiled, looking around, "Alright," he stood up, "Let's get the hell out of here."

We both turned and jumped out of the truck.

I wanted to get out of there as fast as possible. I never wanted to come back to this place either.

"Alright, party's over boys."

CHAPTER 8

My blood went cold like it had so many times before and I turned slowly. About 10 meters away was the lead creature. He had a gun in his hand and it was aimed directly for me. I could see the barrel aimed straight for my chest. I knew that this creature would not hesitate to fire the gun.

"Get in the truck," the creature said, his voice was demanding. I hesitated, unsure. "I said, get in the truck!" His finger tensed around the trigger of the gun. Seeing this movement I turned and climbed up the stairs to the truck. Then two creatures closed the doors behind me. I was trapped. I sat on the floor of the truck. Instead of worrying about myself I worried about Justin. I hoped that he was alright.

I grasped the chain around my neck. There was nothing that I could do about Justin now. I closed my eyes. I rested my head against one of the truck's walls. Why was I so stupid? I knew that they were going to come out sometime, why did I have to wait for so long. I should have gotten out of there faster, we could have left sooner. Why couldn't I have been smarter? Why didn't we leave right away?

A stupid decision will cost you. My dad was talking to me, he was upset, always upset, *it may cost you a life, it may cost you your life, mistakes will happen, Caleb, don't get me wrong, but stupid decisions, those will cost you, you cannot afford any of those*. This was a stupid mistake, a stupid mistake, a stupid-knock… knock, knock…

My eyes flew open, there was only pitch black in front of me, I couldn't see inside the truck. Then I heard a voice, "Caleb? Caleb, are you in there?" The voice came out in a loud whisper and I recognized the voice easily, the thick accent, the soft way he spoke.

"Trithon, yes I am here, why are you here?"

"Caleb, I'm gonna try and get you out of here, okay?"

"No, Trithon, get out of here now!"

"I can't, I need to save you, repay my debt to you!"

"Trithon, get out of here now, if they catch you, they will kill you, leave now, that's an order."

"No, I'm gonna get you out of here!"

"Trithon-" I heard a shot, the noise was so loud that it made me jump. I heard a small intake of breath, "Trithon?" there was no answer, "Trithon, no." I smacked my head against the truck's wall. Then, I crumpled hard on the trucks floor as if I had been shot too. This was all my fault. "Trithon…"

A stupid decision will cost you. A stupid decision will cost you a life. A life that should not have been wasted, a life that should have been protected, that should never have been lost.

"No, Trithon, no, this is all my fault, my fault." My fault, first my father, then the Rangers, then Exterminators, now Trithon. All of these deaths and losses are my fault. Who else am I going to lose along the way?

Voices jolted me back to reality. The voices were coming from outside of the truck. They seemed to be talking about Trithon. The creatures were talking. I leaned my ear against the side of the truck to listen.

"Do you think that this guy was trying to free the human inside of the truck?"

"Definitely," it was the voice of the leader, "the humans are stupid species that have no idea what will happen to them when we win this final war. The general of them is confident, cocky almost. He thinks that he has this war in the bag. He has no idea that we are stronger than humans. We are faster, smarter and we know and will do what we have to do to win this war. We have been waiting for this moment for a long time, all of these years we have been watching the general. The humans will not prevail."

"What about those humans that are smarter, for instance the

humans that have an idea about us?"

"There are not many of those, the humans that have good insight and ideas are shunned from the human community. But the one human that wasn't?" The lead creature laughed, it came out in a cackle.

"The only one that had a lead position in the human Resistance," he spat the word, "We defeated him more than three years ago when the humans were not prepared for an attack." I could tell that the leader was smiling, he's talking about my father, I thought to myself, that is the one that they killed, I felt myself get angry. But I listened as the creature continued.

"None of the humans that went out to protect their community survived so no one ever knew that it wasn't a beast that attacked the community, it was us, the controllers, the rulers of it all."

There was a pause, a silence so great that I could hear my ears ringing. I was confused, but then it all started to make sense. I put together all of the pieces, everything that I learned and everything that I could make up out of this information. My father was not killed by a beast. He wasn't killed by a bug either.

He was murdered. It was a cruel murder by one of these creatures. For all I knew it was the leader standing outside of the truck that had done the killing. For all I knew I could've taken him out. For all I knew I had failed again. They were a smart species, they moved faster and their brains thought faster.

Our general was a coward. He knew that this species was out there but he has faith that they would not be able to take our community down. He thinks that our fighters can withstand this species. Our cowardly general believes that we will survive by doing nothing. He believes that the humans will come out untouched.

I could tell where the general went wrong, he was so greedy for power that he lost control of his surroundings. Now he has himself trapped in his own head, he thinks he can do it but he can't. We can't, humans can't.

Your mind is the strongest element of your body, it controls you. Once your mind gives up, so does your body. Everything can be accomplished if your mind is willing to put aside its pains and act as one with your body. Keep your mind sharp and your thoughts positive, then you will succeed. I could see my father as clear as ever. He was wearing his suit, a commander of an army. He was standing before me, treating me as if I were 18, the age that one can become an officer. I looked down at my hands, they were small for my age of 12, and my head just barely reached my father's lower lip. I stood up tall and straight, excited by the way my father was treating me. I was anxious, yet arrogant. I thought that I was ready.

"If you want to be great then you must go in there and be promoted." I nodded. I thought that I was ready to become an officer, that I was ready to be one of the best. I walked up the steps and opened the general's door without looking back. I remember coming back out. My smile was replaced with a frown. My father's expression hardened and I shook my head, not wanting to tell him. My father grabbed my shoulders and forced my face to look at his.

"I didn't make officer, Sir." My father's expression softened.

"What did you make?"

"Sir, I am promoted to pre-officer." A smile split across my father's face.

"Caleb, you are already my hero." He grabbed my head and forced it into his chest, burying me in a hug. Finally, I felt a smile come across my face, a smile that would stay there for a long time to come. I was my father's hero, his *hero.*

All of a sudden I felt a large jerk, and was awakened back to consciousness. The events that had happened less than an hour before all came back to me. I let my head rest against the truck's cold metal wall. As soon as I put my head back, I felt an upward motion. I felt the truck lifting into the air. All of a sudden it jerked forward and we were off, flying roughly through the sky.

I'm was not sure where the creatures were taking me or if Justin was coming along, or what was going to happen to us but I knew that every second I was getting closer and closer to the creature's compound.

But, as I sat there in the truck, alone, in complete isolation from the rest of the world, negative thoughts started to pour into my brain.

I was captured, probably never going to see Justin or my grandfather again. For all I knew I was riding this truck to my death, and the end of the world, the end of the…world.

My father's words came back into my mind. *Keep your mind sharp and your thoughts positive, then you will succeed.* I could do it. I could think positively and keep my mind sharp. I could save the world.

I was ready. My mind was set. Set only on what I could control, on what I could accomplish. I could take them. I was my father's hero. *I* was my father's hero.

This was my life that I was going to control, this was my world that I was going to set straight, and this was my fight that I was going to win.

I closed my eyes letting myself fall into an uneven sleep.

We had landed no more than an hour ago, now I was sitting on the floor of a metal box, my legs were crossed and my hands were resting softly in my lap. My eyes were closed. They were not closed hard. I could feel my eyelids only resting gently. They were doing nothing more than give me the darkness that I needed in order to do what I was about to do. I needed the darkness so that I could feel free. I needed the darkness to be able to picture where I wanted to be. I needed the darkness to meditate. I was trying to think out this situation, of everything that I could and would do, I could imagine it.

"You should always envision success." My grandfather leaned down towards me. He had a walking stick in hand and a large farmer's hat on his head. His eyes were shielded by the bright sun glaring down and I had to raise my hand to my face to shield the sun so that I could look up at him.

Grandfather continued down the trail that we were walking on, pausing ever so often to look closely at a flower or small plant.

"Grandfather, why do you think that I should envision success?" I was curious, what good is imagining what you want do? Grandfather did not answer for a moment. Instead he leaned down and pointed to a small plant.

"Look closely at this plant, Caleb. Tell me what you see." I crouched down and looked at the plant closely. There was a red flower waiting to bloom but it did not look like the plant had the strength.

"The flower's trapped," I said in shock, looking up at my grandfather's kind and wrinkled face. Grandfather smiled and nodded his head at me. He was asking me to continue. I did as I was told. I looked back at the flower before I spoke again, "The plant is going to die." There was exasperation in my voice.

Grandfather shook his head slowly, "No Caleb, this plant will not die. The plant knows that it is struggling but it will not envision failure. The plant's goal is to live, the plant wants its flower to bloom and its seeds to spread and that is what it will do because it will envision the success. Look here." Grandfather gestured to another flower that was large. Its flower had sprouted and was a beautiful red blossom.

"So, the flower will live?"

Grandfather nodded, "And this is what the flower will look like when it will sprout." He pointed at the beautiful flower again, a smile on his face as wide as the sun is bright.

I felt myself start to smile too, this was perfect.

My brain came back into reality. I could feel the walls of the cell start to close in around me. My body tensed. I was trapped, for now. I knew that they couldn't leave me here for too long. I kept my heart rate slow, breathing in and out of my nose and mouth in five counts, just as my dad had shown me and as Justin did, I could feel my body relaxing, could feel my surroundings start to dissipate and let my brain relax, not thinking, not moving.

I thought of all of my accomplishments, everything that I had done up until this point, I thought of my mistakes. My mistakes held a different meaning to me now, now I could confront them. Now I realized that acknowledging my mistakes would make me stronger, faster and a better fighter over all.

I realized that my struggles had happened over and over again. I realized that to become great you need some failure. Now I was wide awake, life now had a new feeling to me. A new way of living was taking place inside of my head. In that period of time I turned confident, confident that I have made the right decision. I could tell right from wrong.

Then I felt something, something different, a presence. I

was being watched. My eyes snapped open, there were two creatures coming into my cell, both of then wore all white and were carrying guns.

"Come with us." One of the creatures spoke slowly and carefully as if to make sure I could understand him but not startle me.

I stood. My body was working in sync. All of my muscles worked as one, propelling me forward, doing whatever my brain asked of it. One of the creatures walked in front of me, leading the way, the other walked behind me, making sure I didn't wander. As soon as we walked out of my cell four more guards joined us, two of them on each side.

We walked down a long hallway. There were doors every which way. We passed no one along the hall. Finally we reached the end where an elevator stood. The first two guards that had been with me went onto the elevator with me, the other four guards stood where they were. They seemed to be waiting for the doors to close before they would leave. None of the creatures talked as the doors to the elevator closed.

I was standing in between the two creatures. They were gripping their guns tightly. The doors to the elevator opened again and four new guards were standing there, ready to escort me again, I had no idea where we were headed.

Again, two guards accompanied each of my sides and we walked down another hallway. This hallway had sections branching out of each and every side. I looked up and saw that ahead of us was a sign that read, exit. Carefully I slipped a stone from out of one of my suit's pockets and I threw it to my left. It clanked loudly on the metal surface and all of my guards looked in that direction. Their heads whipped around all at the same time, as if in a mechanical fashion.

While their heads were still turned I threw a tracking device on the ground as we passed by the exit. All of the guards looked forward again, recovering from the startling noise. We proceeded down the hall, but what they didn't know was that they were already one step behind me.

We continued further for some more time. We twisted our way through the many hallways that were branching off. Finally, we came to yet another elevator. Again, they forced me on with the other two guards, none of them ever talking. I felt the elevator rise up. This time when the doors opened we came out into a cave. It was a short tunnel no more than 50 meters long. We walked forward and out into an open arena. The stands were full with creatures. All of them were cheering loudly and I was overwhelmed with the sound and tried hard to get back to the state of peace that I was in before.

The guards led me to the center of the arena where a ring and chains came out of the ground. The arena was huge, at least two football fields in both length and width. The stands stretched up into the sky. The ground was hard, dirt covered its surface. I was led to the chains, the guards that were with me chained up my hands. I stood there in the middle of the arena, chained up. The sky was bright. A loud voice started echoing around the arena. I held my breath as I listened to what he said.

"This is a pre-battle for us! Who's ready?" The crowd screamed in delight. I looked around trying to figure out who was doing the talking. "This young man thought that he could infiltrate our base in Russia. He and some of his human friends entered our camp and started eavesdropping. They were caught, being as loud as humans are, and now we have brought them here to entertain us!" The creature speaking yelled the last sentence. All of the creatures in the arena cheered even louder than before.

Then a noise came in through my intercom. A familiar voice, "It's been a really long time, huh?"

I laughed, realizing who it was, "Yes it has, Troy. Do you know what's going on?"

"Nope, no idea," I could sense a hint of humor in Troy's voice.

"Troy."

"Alright fine, you just have to win the battle."

"What battle?"

"They didn't tell you? Oh no, of course they wouldn't."

"Troy." I warned.

"Okay, so you're chained up, right?" I looked at my hands and sighed.

"Yes."

"They are going to send a beast in to fight you."

"What? Troy!"

"I'm not joking." There was no humor left in Troy's voice, "Once you defeat the beast they will try to kill you with all of their powers so you will have to get out of there right away."

I heard rapid typing through the com. "Oh! I see that you are already prepared. Okay, so the exit that you marked leads out into a canyon. I heard more typing, "Yes, at your full speed you will make it, so run at full speed and jump off the cliff. I assume that your suit is still working properly." I looked down at my suit. "Yes," Troy answered for himself. "All that you will have to do is set your suit in the FLY setting. Once you jump just spread your arms and legs and you should be able to fly to the other side."

"Should?"

"Will." Troy confirmed. "Okay, here comes the beast."

I looked at the cave facing me and suddenly a huge beast appeared. It was twice my height. To me it looked like a prehistoric animal. It was what I pictured the other generation of humans "dinosaur" to look like.

The beast had six legs. All of them were armed with claws, huge talons, sharpened for just one purpose, to rip and to tear. Its head was gigantic, longer than me, and its nose stuck out like a muzzle. Five huge rows of sharp teeth lined its gums. Scales covered its whole body like body armor, leaving no gap for anything to penetrate its skin.

It lowered its head and growled at me, sensing a human presence. The legs on its body lined up in rows, three of them. I could tell that it was fast and that this beast wasn't just mutated by the radiation.

I bent down in a fighting position, my chains kept me from doing much but I could still act ready.

"Caleb! Are you stupid?" Troy's voice came out irritated.

"What? No…" I ran my hand through my hair, anxious now.

"Then use your pin, you can get out of those chains." I grabbed the pin from a storage spot right below my left hip. Then I started working on my chains. I stuck my pin into the key holder and then grabbed it into the key slot. Then, I pushed hard and turned. Finally, I heard a click. As the click sounded one of my chains fell off.

Next, I started working on the other one, just as the beast

reared up onto its two back sets of legs. Reared up, it was as tall as a two story house. Its two front legs hit the ground again, thud, thud. It felt like they shook the whole arena. The creatures erupted into even more cheering. All of them were screaming at the tops of their lungs.

"Attention! In this battle the best beast that we have will be facing this human who tried to break into our base. The humans think that they are a stronger power than us but they are wrong! We are stronger and less than five months from now, at this time, we will be raiding the last human Resistance, and finally take Earth for our own."

If possible the arena got even louder. All of the creatures wanted to see me be eaten and turned to sheds. They needed the inspiration and the hope. I finally spotted who was talking, he was on the first level up and his hands were spread wide apart.

A large crown rested on top of his head. I could tell that this was the leader of the creatures. His eyes were bright but there was a coldness there that I could not place. His eyes held a coldness so dark that it seemed like he could easily control the entire world.

He put his hands down and looked at me. Our eyes met, and for an instant, I thought that he knew my story. That he knew who I was and what I was actually doing there. I thought that he knew my name, knew my father's and knew all along what I had come to do. Finally he looked away, his green eyes turned elsewhere. The beast howled and I knew that it was ready, anxious to attack.

I looked back down at my hands, while all of the commotion had been happening I had been busy working on my handcuffs and noticed that the cuffs on both hands had fallen to the ground. They lay there, silver cuffs illuminated against the light brown sand.

"Let the battle, begin!" The lead creature screamed.

I saw one of the creatures jab the beast in the side with a long spear. A creature on the other side of the beast did the same. They were riling the beast up, getting it excited to fight. The creatures were anticipating an easy fight, an easy win over me. The beast charged at me, it was fast, covering the 100 meter distance in a matter of seconds. I was not an easy kill.

Though the beast was fast it was not agile, compared to a human. I easily dodged it the first time, running through his legs as the beast shot by. I stood there with my hands held out in front of me as if I was holding a weapon. My knees were crouched low so that I had good balance, a perfect fighter's stance. Then I felt a short nudge in my side. I pulled out what was bothering me, my cutlass. I breathed a sigh of relief. I could do this with my cutlass.

Seeing only the handle of the cutlass the creatures must not have though that it would be a threat. Just by my thought the double-sided sword appeared. It came out of the handle smoothly. I gripped the cutlass tightly as the crowd erupted into a series of booing. They had wanted me to be an easy kill.

The beast's momentum had carried it almost all the way to the other side of the arena. I saw it slide to a halt. The beast turned, now it was angry. I saw its nostrils flare up, breathing deeply now. It clawed the ground like a bull, ready to charge. I crouched down again, letting my breathing flow in and out, in and out in a steady way. The beast charged again, not so carelessly fast this time.

I hit the ground, sliding underneath the beast as it passed over me. As I slid I stuck out my sword, ripping into the flesh of its back legs. This beast was not used to such combat, it roared in pain as its front legs crumpled to the ground not knowing what else to do. The beast's momentum carried it some more so that the back legs halted when they reached the front legs. It lay there for a moment, the crowd was nearly silent. The creatures were not sure what to do either.

I looked up into the stands and found the leader again. He was leaned over toward someone else, whispering something. I wanted to scream, "Is that all that you got for me? You can do better than that!" Then I had a thought, a memory, this time the memory was asking if it could be seen. I opened up, letting my mind fall into the memory.

"Be careful of what you ask for. Be sure to know what you are wishing for and all of the rights and possibilities. If you fail to understand the meaning of a wish then do not wish at all." My father was standing above me. Then I remembered.

I had said to him that I wished that I could be older, better, stronger and faster. He had told me that some of those wishes could come true with work and perseverance. I agreed to his training program and he had signed me up.

I was a 9 year old, competing and training with 13 and 14 year olds. I remember walking home one night and telling my dad that the training program was too hard, that I was sore and tired and that I didn't want to do it anymore. As soon as I had said those words my father's eyes flared up, scaring me. I had never seen him mad like that.

"Do you want to be great?" He had asked me, there was harshness in his voice that scared me, something so deep that it frightened me thoroughly.

"What?" My frightened mind could not place what he had said.

"Do you want to be great?" My father had raised his voice.

"Yes," I managed to squeak out.

"Really? Well it doesn't seem like it!"

I had never seen my father this angry except for the time when he learned that my brother, Justin, had stayed out past curfew. I remembered him towering over my brother like a lion ready to pounce. Justin had been cringing underneath him, scared of what he might do.

"If you want to be great then you have to complete this training program! If you want to be great then you must go the extra mile. If you want to be great then you have to fight every battle like it's your last. If you want to be great then you have to want it more than your opponent. If you want to be great then you must train when no one is watching and work while your opponents rest. If you want to be great you must do it yourself. You will not be great unless you work harder than you think you can."

My father was breathing hard. I was staring at him in awe. My father leaned over and sat hard on the cold winter ground. He put his face in his hands.

"Father," I paused, and sat down with him, "Sir, I do want to be great. I want to be greater than brother. I want to be greater than you." Father looked up. He put one of his hands on my back.

"Caleb," all of the anger was gone from his face, it was replaced with a sparkle, a twinkle was in his eye, "You will be greater than me, you will be greater than your brother, you will be greater than Grandfather, you will be the best fighter to have walked this Earth if you put your sword up and fight."

That's when he pulled out a package. It was small but when he handed it over to me it felt heavier than it should have for its size. "This is for you. I was meaning to save it for Christmas but now seems like an appropriate and right time." I held the package in my hands for a moment, "Well go on, son. Open it."

I gripped the package tighter and torn into the cylinder. There in my hands was a cutlass handle, I gasped. Father laughed.

"The more that you use it the more in tune, or synced it will be to your brain." I held it like it was going to be taken away from me the next second. I never wanted to let it go. I sat there for a long while. Just being in the presence of my father was soothing and I felt my stress wash away.

Slowly, the memory dispersed. I was back in the present, holding onto my cutlass tightly. My vision was now sharper. It was like I could see every single creature in the stands, my hearing was better, I could separate voices. I could tell which was a chief or general. My eyes focused on the cave that the beast before had came out of. I could tell that there was something greater, another beast ready to come out of this cave.

"Troy? Do you know what is happening?"

"Umm, I can kind of get the idea…" Troy paused.

"Which is?"

"I can tell that the leader is for one, mad that you defeated that beast, and for two mad that his guards let you get in with your cutlass. So, he's gonna send in another beast maybe multiple, to wipe you out completely. He's embarrassed. Be ready for the worst." Troy's voice sounded flat, but I could read the fear etched in his voice, the fear that was rarely there. I took a deep breath.

"Will there be more than one?"

"Probably, most likely, definitely," Troy managed to gulp, he swallowed hard. I took a deep breath too. My mind was running fast.

There was a pause. Then Troy spoke again. "Caleb? My scanners are sensing a shift of power. The beasts are almost ready to attack." I looked up into the starry night. The crowd was almost quiet but none of them were leaving their seats. They were ready. I looked at the leader. He was sitting back in his chair resting his head. There was a smile stretched across his face. He was excited, happy to get rid of one more human, one more man to stand in the way of conquering the world and he was going to do it in a fashion to excite the rest of his army, to get them ready for the battle.

I shifted my weight, sensing another presence. A presence of a beast. Finally a head emerged from the mouth of a cave. The head was wide and the mouth was lined with razor sharp teeth. A line of spikes traveled down its back and spine. It was smaller than me but it looked quicker and more agile. It also looked ready to give itself up at all cost. Another beast exactly like it came out of the cave behind it, then another. A total of three beasts exited the cave. They stood there part wolverine-part cheetah, snarling at me, waiting for their command to attack me and rip me to shreds and pieces.

I could feel my heart rate begin to quicken. I could tell that I was beginning to fear. My breath was coming out faster, *control* I thought to myself. *You can control your fear and these beasts*. The beasts began to circle each other. They were snarling, slobbering all over. I could see the saliva from where I stood, 100 meters away.

"You have fought bravely, human," the leader of the creatures snarled when he said the word human, he laughed, "but now you are going to die. Send in the beasts!"

The leader roared and threw up his hands. Two guards on either side of the wolverine cheetahs jabbed one of them to start the fight. It howled and turned, looked at one of the guards and then lunged, swallowing a guard in one gulp.

Then it screamed into the night sky. The beasts began to circle again but this time, there was a more agitated step in the way they walked, it was faster. I could tell that they were beginning to eye me up. They were figuring out the best way to take me down.

Holding my cutlass I got into a stance.

I saw one of the wolverine cheetahs arch its shoulders and spring into a sprint, the other two followed close behind. I held my ground in the center of the arena. I waited, waited for the right time. The creatures ran fast. They were smart too. I could see it in their eyes, the way that they moved, as a pack instead of separate.

Both of their eyes were centered at the fronts of their heads. The eyes were meant for predators, they were the king beast. Just like humans. Unlike humans fur blocked any peripheral vision. I was going to use that one disability to my advantage.

As soon as they were about 25 meters away I took three long strides towards the closest beast. Using my momentum I leaped into the air. Holding my cutlass out in front of me I easily smacked the two beasts on either side of the middle beast. The middle wolverine cheetah had slowed down allowing the others to pass and I had seen my opportunity to attack. None the less, I knew that the wolverine cheetahs would get back to their feet and join the battle again.

Now, the two wolverine cheetahs fell hard to the ground. I sheathed my cutlass in a smooth motion. While still in the air I brought my fist back to my side gathering my strength. Time seemed to slow. I waited, waited until the beast had leaped into the air. Its eyes were glazed over and I could barely see my reflection in its dark black pupils.

A surge of anger went through my body when I remembered my father's face, his kind eyes, and his knowing smile. I yelled out in pain, internal pain. With renewed strength I let my fist fly forward with all of my might. I felt the spikes sprout from the suit's knuckles just as my hand collided with the beast's face. This time, I was ready for the pain. I held my hand firm. I felt my teeth grind together as to not yell out.

I felt the wolverine cheetah's jaw dislocate underneath my strength, power and the sharpness of my suit. The monster fell to the ground, hard. I landed too. Gracefully I came up into a battle stance. I grabbed my cutlass from my sheath and the double-sided blade extended out.

I turned and faced my next two opponents. I faced the opponents that I had already hit and taken out before. They were looking at me. I could tell that they were interested in the way I fought.

I could see the fear in their bodies. I did not know if they would have the courage to attack. Then one of them jumped, I lashed out and struck it with the sharp side of my blade. It fell to the ground.

The other wolverine cheetah had jumped as well. I jumped into the air, spinning as my leg swung around colliding with the beast's face, my momentum kept carrying me forward and my other leg followed close behind, kicking the beast again. That beast fell to the ground too.

Stillness came across the night. I looked up. I was not sure what to expect, but to expect something big. I did not know why I had this feeling but the feeling was so strong that I knew something would happen.

My eyes started scanning the sky. They should be here soon, I thought to myself. As soon as I said the thought in my mind a couple thousand men and women fell from the sky. Gunfire immediately lit up the night along with shouts from the creatures. They were here.

As soon as the men landed, chaos broke loose. The lead creature immediately sent in the guards. I heard the swords clash, and the guns go off. I saw creatures fall and men fall. I was at the center of it. *It's finally happening.* I smiled. *It was the start of the rebellion.*

CHAPTER 9

"Men are falling! These creatures are much too strong for our forces! We must fall back!" A man that had been fighting beside me who seemed like a leader yelled to me. I turned to look at him. His black face turned my way and I saw the fear in his eyes.

"No!" I yelled back, "we cannot let them know that we are afraid. Your soldiers must think that we will win, otherwise there is no way!" The general nodded. Immediately after he did so his dark eyes flashed.

"Duck!" he yelled. I dropped to the ground just as the general threw one of his double-sided axes straight over my head. It nailed the creature in the forehead and stuck there. The creature fell to the ground. I stood.

Then, I grabbed my cutlass and entered the battle. I clashed arms with a creature who had already been hit. He was easy. All it took to defeat him was a jab and a swing and he was gone. I forged ahead, clashing arms with creatures every so often. I looked up into the arena stands and found my target, the leader of the creatures. He was staring down at the battle. It looked like he was analyzing.

I ran at full speed towards where the leader was standing, three creatures surrounded him. They were protecting him. I could tell that they would not let anything happen to him and always stand in the way.

I jumped into the air, but as soon as I jumped I knew that it would not be far enough. I pushed a button on my suit that extended out my suit fabric and material. Then I stretched out my arms. I felt the air catch in the extended fabric and I pushed my arms down hard. I felt myself rise higher into the air.

I landed softly on the stands right beside the leader. As soon as I landed I pointed my cutlass out so that it rested across his throat. All three of his men turned, one had a gun, and the other two had swords.

"Now I see it." The leader shook his head back and forth, back and forth, he looked into my eyes. There was no fear there. "I cannot believe that I did not see it earlier." The creature continued slowly.

He was so human-like that it was hard to tell. His blonde hair hung slightly over his eyes. His eyes were such a dark green that they looked soulless. The way he moved was the only way to tell what he really was, just like all of the other creatures. His eyes shifted back and forth, faster than a human's.

He did not seem to mind my cutlass digging into his neck. "All of the bits and pieces are coming together for me now. You were their leader." He pointed his finger at me, looking at me in shock. Or was it amusement?

"What did you think?" I snarled.

"I thought that we had you. I thought that you were just another human. I thought that we could use you to rile up the creatures." The leader smiled. The smile was filled with hate and despise. "I guess not."

The leader raised his hand into the air. His palm was cupped. Without warning, he yelled, "this is what I must do, for the new era of mankind, a different type of man, the *fast man*!" The creature brought down his hand.

The creature with the gun immediately started firing. I had anticipated this move from the leader, but not the skill of the creature. I jumped into the air, dodging all of the bullets that were aimed directly for me. The firing of the bullets increased. One grazed my leg but I clenched my teeth to not show the pain. Then, I turned and jumped off the arena stands. I fell hard onto the ground below. The leader sent the creature after me. As I landed I turned and watched as the creature jumped into the air.

He landed softly on the hard ground. As soon as his feet

touched the ground he pointed his gun out. It was aimed directly towards me. I could see the tension in his fingers, could see his thumb tighten and his finger tighten around the trigger. I could see the sweat on his brow. I could see the human in him, all of the human.

I was not going to die today. I ran forward with two large steps, and saw his finger clench, pulling the trigger. I slid and the bullet whizzed over my head. I stood again and saw where the gun was aimed for this time, my left hip.

As soon as I saw the gun's barrel I dodged to the right and kept running, straight towards the creature. I grabbed my cutlass from behind my back and leaped. All at once, I saw him pull the trigger for the last time. My sword's blade moved immediately into the bullet's path and deflected the bullet away from my body. I quickly turned my blade so it pointed downward. The blade sunk into the creature's chest.

I looked up. The leader of the creatures was looking down in disgust. The leader abruptly turned and, accompanied by his two bodyguards, walked away from the battle. He wanted to save himself.

I turned. Jets were flying in from all around. As I watched I saw one of the jets get hit with a bullet in the right wing. Another bullet followed close behind, and seconds later they hit their target. The jet exploded in a wave of fire. I could feel the heat on my face. The heat was like I had never felt before. It was as if a dragon had blown fire no more than 50 meters away from me. I watched as parts of the jet spiraled down towards the ground. Each part fell in large heaps onto the ground. The battle raged on. I saw men fall to the creatures. We were outnumbered and outmatched.

Without time to think, I heard a whizzing noise and then I felt pain. The pain was taking place in my right thigh. The pain was so great that I fell to the ground, crying out. I looked down. A bullet had gone right through my suit. I saw the blood. It was gushing out.

Then, I felt a hand on my shoulder. I looked up into a man's face. He wore a white suit, a doctor. He was screaming at someone behind him. All of the noises seemed to blur together. Then there was silence and my eyes closed, the last sound that I heard was the firing, the firing and the yelling of men as they fell.

I felt my body being lifted into the air and then placed both carefully and gently onto a stretcher. I felt the stretcher being lifted into the air. I stared up into the sky. The stars were out. I could count about two dozen in the night. I could see all of the clouds.

Those are not clouds, son, those clouds that you speak of are the pollution. The pollution left by our ancestors, we were careless and we still are. We are greedy, the stars... are not. My father's voice came back to me in my mind, clearly and effortlessly. I could hear despise in his voice, the way he loathed human nature. I looked up at the stars. They twinkled down at me. Their beauty brought a smile to my lips.

Suddenly, the stretcher shifted and I was almost thrown off. I looked around, panicking. My leg was now stinging again. It was a pain so unreal that I let out a faint yell. I saw one of the men carrying the stretcher fall to the ground. Another man stepped up in his place and we started moving again, this time faster. Finally, we made it to wherever we were headed. I could still hear the battle cries from around me, if anything, they had intensified. I was lifted into a jet. Before I could say anything else the jet took off from the ground.

I tried to sit up but the pain in my leg intensified. A man walked out of the ship's cockpit. His skin was a dark brown color, he was very tall and he held himself up with strength and courage, *the general.*

"General. What an honor," I held out my hand, and winced in pain with the movement.

"My name is James Johnson." The general told me, "I am the general of a Resistance. Our Resistance is made up of people that were banished from the North American Resistance. We believe in fighting the creatures as I am sure that you do." The general smiled at me.

"My name is Caleb Hanson." I winced as pain shot through my body, "You are right, I do believe in fighting the creatures. I had no idea that there was another Resistance though."

General Johnson nodded, "Yes, we are one of the other Resistances that still fights back, everyone else has..." The general looked into my eyes. There was pain there at a memory. "Everyone else has... given up."

Someone stepped out of the cockpit behind the general.

She had long, golden brown hair and bright blue eyes. She was tall, about the same height as the general was, probably five feet and eleven inches.

"And you are?" I looked into her eyes as I asked her the question. They were like the sea, stretching out endlessly before me. I could not look away.

"Jami Kearns," she said. She made no movement to hold out her hand. She just tossed her head to the side a little, making her hair wave with the motion. "I'm the Director of Training for our group." Her eyes twinkled.

I leaned back in the chair and immediately regretted the decision. I winced in pain.

"Get him to the infirmary." The general's smooth as caramel voice spoke across the jet. The general turned to Jami as a doctor moved to grab my bed. I laid my head back down on my pillow and closed my eyes. "Kearns, suit up, we are going in."

"Yes, Sir," she responded. I could hear the smile in her voice. She was ready for battle. Then my mind went blank.

No more thinking. No more fighting. No more pain, just… emptiness. My mind didn't try to think. It didn't try to react. I just lay there, no thoughts. There was nothing. My mind was too tired to go searching, all I wanted to do was lay there. Lay there and forget, just forget everything. My body relaxed. I felt my tense muscles finally disengage from the stress of battle. I felt my mind rest, finally at ease. Then it went completely blank.

I woke up to searing pain coursing through my body. The pain was so great that I yelled out. My hands clutched solid material and squeezed on tight. I couldn't let go.

Instead of focusing on the pain I made my brain focus on breathing. My brain struggled to focus but I kept trying. I focused on breathing in and out through my nose and through my mouth. The breathing momentarily distracted me from the pain and I felt my brain start to shut down, until I could not think, could not move, *what is happening to me?*

"Doc," I heard a voice, it sounded very distant to my ears. I could feel a presence close, "Doc, I think that he is awake." The voice was soft, it was smooth and light. I could feel myself relax.

"Put him back under, we are not done with him yet." The voice of the doctor was gruff. It was a man's voice.

"Yes, Sir," I felt movement.

Then I felt nothing, I was out.

I must have fallen asleep because I woke to the sound of a door closing. My eyelids fluttered open and I found myself in a circular shaped room. The room was dark and it had a dank smell to it, like I was underground. The walls were a dark shade of gray. There were no windows. In the far corner of the room there was a small bathroom with a sink and tub. My eyes focused on the person who had entered my room.

He was tall, taller than me. He had short brown hair and deep brown eyes. I recognized him immediately.

"Justin," I breathed. I moved to sit up but was faced with a pounding in my head. Justin's large smile quickly changed to a frown.

"What's wrong?" His eyebrows furrowed together and rose. I knew he was concerned. I made myself sit up, ignoring the pain in my leg and the pounding in my head. I made myself smile.

"I'm fine," I said with a grimace, "what about you?"

"I'm good," Justin said quickly, he still looked concerned for me. It looked like he did not believe what I had said. He continued, "Those creatures didn't do much to me, all they did was force me to sit in a room. Then, Troy came in through my earpiece and told me that the door was open. I just got up and walked through the door. A bunch of men met me outside of the door. Then, they took me here. I kept asking about you and they said that you would live." Justin paused. He looked at me, "What happened to you?"

I hesitated. I was unsure how to answer. "I… I fought a beast and killed it," I stated it like fact. My voice sounded dull to my ears. I paused, "Then, then they sent in three beasts. I took all of them out, just as the men started falling from the sky. A large battle occurred and I was shot in the leg." I buried my face in my hands, remembering the experience, "Where are we?"

"We are in their headquarters. I heard that it was the last Resistance still fighting. Do you believe it?" Justin sat at the foot of my bed, shaking his head back and forth.

"Yes," I said, "I do believe it."

Justin looked at me with surprise on his face. I did not look away. Finally, he continued speaking, "We are underground because the beasts and creatures claimed the area above us. They call themselves 'The last of the Resistance'." He sounded disgusted.

"I think that they are right." I said again. Justin looked at me incredulously, "the general is just waiting, not attacking. He does not think that the creatures will come for him if he never attacks them. I thought he was right for some time, but now I can see how wrong he is. They are coming for him last. They are now stronger than ever. They do not plan to share our world. Their nature is a lot like the human's." I sighed running my hand through my curly blond hair. "Who are these people anyways?"

"Resistance escapees, people who were sent out by the Resistance, unneeded and unwanted," Justin bit his lower lip. He looked nervous.

"That is what I heard but I did not believe it at first." I said to Justin, "I can't believe that the Resistance would send people away."

"There is a lot that I do not believe about the Resistance now." Justin sighed. He looked older. It was as if his experiences had aged him. "What do you think will happen to us, Caleb, what will happen to our world?"

Everything became real to me again, the battle, all of the fights, the loss of Trithon. My hands started shaking and I ran my right hand through my hair to hide their shakiness, I clutched my left hand so tightly at my side that my fingers turned white.

"I don't know," I answered truthfully. Justin sighed. I stood, slowly and carefully. I waited until my vision cleared to do more. There was a loud knock on my door.

"Dinner time," a voice from the other side of the door yelled.

"You get cleaned up," Justin said, looking me up and down, "I'll meet you at the dining hall. I gave a curt nod as Justin walked slowly to the door. He turned at the door and looked back at me. Then he smiled, "Glad to see you again, Caleb."

I forced a smile back. He nodded, and then left.

As soon as he was gone I sat back down on the bed, hard. I put my face in my hands, focusing on my breathing. *Three seconds,* I told myself, *and then you must move on.* One……. Two……. *Three.*

I stared at my sandwich that was beside a glass of water. All around me people were talking. They were yelling loudly at one another. They were throwing food. They were laughing and having a good time. I was at a table by myself. It's a community, I thought, just like the Resistance. Just like home.

It had been a long time since I had thought of home. Now, home seemed more like a memory than reality. I just couldn't bring myself to believe that it was gone. I could bring myself to believe that I wasn't going back. But I did think of home now. I thought of home now that I was alone, now that I was in a strange new space.

I remembered the smell of sweet lemongrass that I would inhale when I set my foot in the door. The bright lighting and the laughing and talking of my family once I had gotten home from school.

I pictured my mother and her elegance. I pictured the way she spoke and talked and walked. Justin looked the most like her, their smile and ears were the same. Their hair was the same color too. It was a light brown.

I pictured my father. We looked almost exactly alike. We had dirty blonde hair. Our hair was curly. What set us apart from everyone else were our eyes. Our eyes were green, a bright green. Our ears were the same as well. They stuck out, just a bit from the side of my head. I missed my mother and father now, now that I wouldn't be seeing them for some time. I could feel the tears. I knew that they would not come. I could hold them back. I had done so for this long.

"Caleb, you must eat." A harsh voice came into my mind, looking up I saw my father. He was frowning down at me, a look that I had gotten used to.

There was movement in front of me. I looked up to see Justin. He looked down at me and smiled.

"Hey." Justin sat down in front of me. I nodded back at

him as he slid into the seat across from me.

Justin seemed… happy.

"What's up?"

Justin hesitated, and then smiled. "You see that woman over there?" Justin pointed at Jami.

She was seated across from the general, laughing at something that she said. I turned away in disgust. Or was it something else. Was it something other than disgust? Was it… jealousy?

I look a bite out of my sandwich. It tasted dry in my mouth. The bread seemed stale. "I've got to go." I spoke quickly. I stood up.

Justin didn't respond. Instead, he kept staring at Jami, watching her every move. I sighed. Then I left. I slowly made my way back to my room. Why was I angry at Justin? Was it jealously?

I shook those thoughts away. I had to forget about Jami. Justin was my brother, and nothing was going to break apart the friendship that we had. I paused at my bedroom door. *Or could Jami?*

CHAPTER 10

I was standing in the middle of my room. The walls were dark gray just like before. Nothing had changed except for the stack of my gray and black clothes that were stacked in a pile at the foot of my bed. I dropped to the bed hard and rested my head in my hands.

My bed was not uncomfortable but I could not fall asleep. I kept hearing the screams and cries of the soldiers going down. I replayed my battles with the beasts over and over again in my head, assessing my tactics. Suddenly my room shook. It did not shake hard enough to be an earthquake but I sat up, looking around. I could hear my heart thumping in my chest hard just as an alarm started blaring throughout the Resistance.

Before I knew it I was up, grabbing my cutlass and throwing on a shirt. I tore out into the hallway and was immediately engulfed in a crowd of people of the Resistance. Soldiers were standing everywhere.

They were motioning the people to a safe destination. I stuck to the wall by my bedroom door trying to make my way the opposite direction of where everyone else was going. Finally, I found a gap in the crowd. I took the gap in the crowd and came to a barrier.

Soldiers were working on it. They looked like they were trying to make it strong. They were trying to make it strong enough to protect against something. By the way they were barricading it looked like that something was very large and strong. I grabbed one of the soldier's arms and pulled him towards me. He struggled against my grip but I was too strong.

"Tell me what's going on." My voice was so demanding that it even surprised me.

"I… I don't know," the soldier's voice shook and his eyes glanced around nervously.

"Tell me everything that you know," I shook his arm hard. His eyes stared up at me in terror. Realizing my mistake I released my grip. I shook my hair out of my eyes and tried again, "What do you know?"

The soldier swallowed hard, then spoke, "There was a break-in, I… I was told to barricade this entrance…" I was gone before he could finish.

I ran past the blaring alarms. I was searching for something but not sure what. I ran past doors and finally found one that had been blasted out of the way. I quickly stepped through and finally heard the sounds of the swords clashing, of guns firing, and of people screaming. I dodged glass and wood and splinters as I ran. I ran, not looking back. I ran towards the sounds of the battle. Finally, I reached the fight.

The general was in the center of the room taking on a group of five creatures with the help of a woman. I caught a glimpse of the woman for a second. She has long golden hair that was pulled back and out of her face. Her eyes are a sharp blue, like the ocean. *Jami*, I automatically relaxed though I was not sure why. I stepped into the fight, taking down creatures slowly along with the others.

"We have to fall back!" The general's eyes found mine. The creatures were too strong. I looked around the room at the other fighters. Justin was in the corner fighting a beast of his own. There were only three other fighters. They were all fighting towards the exit. I nodded my head. We were much too outnumbered.

"Fall back!" I yelled loudly. Justin met my gaze and I nodded. He pulled his sword from the beast that he was fighting and grabbed a soldier that was nearest to him as he exited. Jami followed him along with the other soldiers that were still standing. The general exited next. He took down one final creature before he left. I followed close behind. I slammed the door behind me and locked it.

"We don't have much time," the General Johnson said as

he took off his blood-stained coat. “We must move fast if we want to keep the rest of our Resistance.” He threw his coat to the ground and then took off again. This time he traveled at a fast run. He started moving right as I heard banging on the door.

Minutes later we were standing in a room with a map of the Resistance stretched out before us.

“The creatures have taken over the entire west and central portions of the Resistance. That means that what we have left is only on the outskirts. I know of some passages that can lead us out of here but I am not about to leave our children and non-soldiers defenseless.” Jami and the other three nodded as I did. Justin looked around the room and after a moment’s hesitation, he nodded as well.

The general paused, waiting for our response. His dark eyes had lost the twinkle that they had before. Now they were dull. They had no gleam. They did not even have ambition. His eyes were just… blank.

“Alright,” the general’s voice sounded strained. He was holding back. I tried to meet his eyes but he turned away, “Let’s go save our Resistance!”

He threw his hand into the center of our circle. Jami and the other three warriors followed. The act was so childish that it almost made me smile.

Almost.

I put my hand in the center so that it rested on top of Jami’s. Her hand was cold but it sent energy through my body. She met my gaze. Her blue eyes were so piercing that they shot right to my soul. She tried to smile, but it did not reach her eyes. I nodded.

“Caleb, you and Justin will take the southwest side of the Resistance. Try to find anyone that was left behind and secure that wing. If you find anyone bring them to the north side, which is where our safe house is set up.” I nodded at his words. Then I grabbed my cutlass. I was ready to fight for what I loved. I was ready to die for what I loved.

I felt a strong hand grab my arm. It was cold but smooth. I turned and let Jami lead me away from the group. She turned and looked at me. Her eyes held mine for a moment and then looked away.

“Caleb, you have to be careful. These creatures are strong.”

She looked back up at me again and her bright blues eyes sent waves of energy through my body. I nodded my head, not knowing what to say. I was frozen in her eyes. “Just, please do not get hurt.” Her blue eyes begged me.

I did not anticipate her next move. She stood on her toes and leaned towards me, she pressed her lips against my cheek. Unlike her hands, her lips were warm. Without another word she turned and walked back to the map and the general. Energy coursed through my body, like a wave, growing bigger and bigger. I was ready to fight. I turned and walked quickly out of the room.

It took me a moment to realize that Justin was lagging behind. I turned and saw a look on his face that I had never seen before, fear? No, not fear. Anger?

“Justin, what’s wrong?”

“Nothing is wrong, okay?” He continued quickly onward. I had to run to catch up to his fast pace. His eyes were set on the path ahead.

I grabbed his shoulder and made him face me. His eyes blazed with anger. He looked away from me again.

“Justin, what are you doing?” He barely gave me time to finish this sentence. His angry eyes looked at me hard again.

“No, Caleb. What are you doing?” His shoulders were shaking with anger and the hatred in his voice scared me.

“I… I, what? What are you talking about?” I felt confusion blast through my body. What was he angry about?

Justin turned away and continued walking down the path to the southwest side of the Resistance, “”You knew I liked her...” His voice was barely audible, “and yet, you still went for her.”

Justin did not look at me as he spoke. Alternatively, he continued forward. Onward down the path. He seemed to want to be as far away from me as possible. A feeling like no other flew through me. Something bad was about to happen.

“Justin-” Justin started to turn back towards me as a beast flew out from the side of the path and landed on Justin’s back. He yelled as the beast threw back his clawed hand. It was ready to strike.

“No!” I leaped forward. I threw one of my knives at the beast, the knife lodged into the beast’s skin. I could make it to the beast in time, I had to. I took two more steps forward. I saw the beast's arm.

It was making its downward motion towards Justin's head. He was struggling but he was not strong enough to shake the beast off of himself. I didn't have time to think of what I was doing. I didn't have time to plan how I was going to do it. All I knew was Justin was not going to die today.

I took one more step forward and then I threw myself into the path of the beast's arm prepared to land on top of Justin. I grabbed my cutlass as I jumped and held it out in front of me. As I jumped I closed my eyes, my life flashed before me.

I saw myself as a little kid. Nothing could get in my way. I saw my father, he was standing beside my mother and brother, Justin, pleased with what he saw in me. I saw my grandfather. I saw his expectations of me to do great. His smile. Then, I saw Justin. I saw us together as children. I saw us play. I saw us fight. But most of all I saw us have each other's backs. Always.

I came back into the present. Why wasn't I dead? A muffled groan came from underneath me. I stared straight ahead, not believing what I saw. The beast was stuck at the end of my cutlass. Its hand was down at its side and its mouth hung open, just slightly. The bear-like beast was dead.

"Get offa me," quickly, I stood and looked down. Justin lay on the ground below me. His face was red and he was breathing hard.

I smiled, offering him my hand. He looked away and got up by himself. Then I remembered, Jami. A stern expression was on his features.

"Justin…"

"We have to move," he would not meet my eyes. I felt a sinking feeling in my stomach, "we must make it to the southwest side of the Resistance. The longer we take, the more the creatures take over, the longer we take…"

"Justin," I stepped in front of him, blocking him off. He looked away. "Justin, I'm so sorry." I shook my head back and forth as my shaggy blond hair swung side to side.

"I bet that you are." Justin shoved past me and made his way down the hall.

"Justin, wait."

"We have to move." Justin picked up the pace. I had no choice but to follow him.

About fifteen minutes later of walking in silence we were at the entrance of the southwest side of the Resistance. Justin stopped and looked up at the sign above the door. It read southwest side in large rustic letters. Justin turned around and his dark brown eyes met mine. They held for a moment and then looked away. My heart sank. I was going to get him back, somehow. I knew that I would.

Justin stepped through the door and I followed close behind him. The walls were a darker gray than the walls before. Doors led off every which direction from the main hall. We kept to the center. We slowly made our way down the long hallway.

"That's weird," I heard myself say, "no one is here, you would think that someone or something should be here."

I heard Justin grunt in response. It was as if I was so much lower than him that he couldn't even speak to me. We turned a corner and hit a dead end.

"Where is everyone?" I asked turning around in a circle. Justin didn't answer. I looked up but didn't see him anywhere. "Justin?" I asked.

Suddenly, I heard a noise, a creaking of a door. I spun around and saw Justin helping a small boy and his family down some steps that had been smashed aside. The boy's face was streaked with mud and tears and his parents were both shaking. I raced to Justin's side and spread out my arms.

"It's okay." I said calmly, "you can jump." I told the boy, "I'll catch you." The boy nodded and leapt into my arms. I caught him in the air and gently set him on the ground beside me. I turned again and helped down his mother. His father jumped down himself and I grabbed his shoulder to steady him.

"Thanks," he said weakly and smiled slightly at me. I gave a quick nod.

"Do you know of anyone else that lives in these parts of the Resistance?" I asked the man. He nodded.

"Many people do, they must have cleared out when the…

those creatures came blasting in…" he took a deep breath and then continued, "there was an elderly couple living in that room," the man pointed across the hall with a shaky finger. I nodded twice, thanking him and then I turned.

"Justin, lead this family back to the north side. If you find anyone else bring them with you. I should be there as soon as I can, I'm only going to secure this perimeter and make sure no one else is out here." Justin was already shaking his head, back and forth, ever so slightly. No, he mouthed to me, "Justin that is an order," I looked into his eyes sharply, begging him to do as I told.

Justin stepped forward and put his hand on my shoulder, and then he pulled me into his body, into a hug. I slowly extended my arm around him too.

"I'm sorry," Justin spoke slowly and in a low voice, "be safe little bro."

"I'm sorry too." I pulled back and smiled. After a moment he smiled back. Then, he turned and made his way back down the hall.

"Let's go." He motioned for the family to follow him and the little boy led the way, right out the door.

As they exited the mom leaned down towards the boy and the boy reached up, standing on his toes. It was as if he wanted to tell her something. His whispered words drifted to my ears. His voice was soft.

"Mommy, when I get older, I want to be just like that guy back there." He pointed back to me and I smiled.

"You can be anything you want to be, Jakey, you just have to work hard. If you do, you can be exactly like him." Jakey smiled and the mom leaned away. Soon they were out of sight, away from their home. After a second's pause, I turned. I walked into the room that was the home of the elderly couple.

The room was dark, and smelled old, like something had crawled in there and died. The door creaked as I pushed it aside. In the front room there was nothing, only a bench and some shoes. I turned a corner and saw the living room. There were no signs of human life. I held my cutlass out in front of me prepared for anything.

On the couch was a creature. He was just sitting there waiting for something. He had his head down and was reading what looked like a magazine. As I entered the room he looked up, then a huge smile lit his face.

"Ah, Caleb Hanson, we have been expecting you…" his voice came out raspy. I froze. How did he know my name? "Welcome, human leader, to the home of me and my men!" As he said those last words three creatures stepped up behind me blocking my exit, and two creatures stepped up on either side of me.

"This is not your home to take." I growled at the creature, "and you are no man."

"I am more man than you think." The creature said softly, his eyes flickered about. He paused, looking around the room, "Well, if this is not my home, whose home is it?" The creature grinned. There was a mischievous look on his face.

"This home belongs to an old couple. They live here." I said slowly, never taking my eyes off of the creature. The creature laughed.

"Them?" he cackled, "You think we would let you pesky humans take control of our territory!" His eyes shifted back and forth. They flickered faster than a human's would. With those words the two creatures behind me stepped up. Their swords were poised at the ready. They wanted me out.

I tensed, sensing a battle approaching.

"Now, all I have to do is kill you, Hanson. All I have to do is kill their leader, and we shall win this war against your human friends." He sneered. Suddenly hot anger boiled up inside of me. My muscles ached for a battle. I gave my muscles what they craved.

CHAPTER 11

"You fool!" The creature screamed. The creature kicked me in the side of the head. He advanced on me as I fell to the floor. "This is not how I want you to die!" The creature was breathing hard.

My hands were tied back behind my back. I tasted blood in my mouth and vaguely remembered the fight. I remembered lunging backwards with my cutlass and taking out at least eight creatures. I also remembered lashing out at the creature that seemed to be the leader of this pack.

I looked up. Yes, the lead creature had a swollen jaw and also the start of a black eye. I smiled at my small victory.

The creature advanced on me again and kicked me hard in my stomach. I groaned and rolled over. The creature kicked me again. This time I curled into a ball, protecting my stomach and my head.

"Get up," the creature growled. I didn't move. Alternately, I stayed where I was. I stayed curled up as small as I could be. "I said, get up!" The creature grabbed the edge of my shirt and pulled me to my feet. It punched me in the stomach again. This time I groaned in agony.

"Or else what?" I managed. My breath was coming out in short breaths. I was struggling to stay conscious as my mind began to waver. "You'll kill me?" I managed to ask. I felt myself chuckle. My brain was acting slower now. I had to conserve energy. I had to stay awake.

The creature dropped me to the ground. Again, I lost my footing and fell. I looked up as the creature leaned down. Its breath smelled stale and its eyes flickered back and forth, fast. It looked nervous and… embarrassed.

"You do not question my authority." The creature drew back his leg and kicked me again. I felt all of the breath leave my body and lay there, gasping for air. The leader turned to the other creatures surrounding me. "Take him out the back and deposit him, we do not need him anymore, he will only become another issue, another threat to our hold on the world."

The creatures nodded at their leader's words, as if in agreement. However, they made no movement towards me. I smiled at their stress. The lead creature looked frustrated. "Go!" The leader snarled.

I was immediately surrounded by creatures. They grabbed me and heaved me up. They set me on my feet and shoved me forward. I stumbled, but this time I did not fall.

"Let go of me," I growled at the creatures as their hands settled on my back shoving me forward. I stumbled forward as the creatures led me out a door. The outdoor air hit me hard and I was taken aback by how bright the sun was. Momentarily blinded, I let the creatures lead me to my spot of execution. The outdoors…

I did not think that it would happen like this. My death. I thought that it would happen in a battle. That I would be fighting for what I loved. *This is what I love.* A voice inside my head spoke to me. I am fighting for my world, for my family, for my grandfather, and for my father. My father.

"He would be proud of you now." My grandfather's voice came back to me. He was proud. I realized that I could hear the strain in his voice. I could hear the strain in his voice that only occurred when he did not fully believe what he was saying.

I grasped the chain around my neck as the creatures kicked my legs out from under me. I fell to my knees. I held onto the chain harder, *do not let go*. My father's words came back to me and this time I understood what they meant for a different reason than I usually understood them for, *do not let go.*

I heard the creature take out his gun and train it on my head. I heard the click of the bullet sliding into place. *I do not want to die.*

I am not going to die today.

I leapt to my feet and kneed the creature with the gun in the stomach. The impact was so hard that I knew he was not going to get back up. He grunted and dropped the gun, falling to the ground. I turned around and kicked another creature to the ground. As I did so, I felt the bindings behind my back break. My hands were free.

I grabbed a gun and fired off shots, taking the creatures down, one by one. Suddenly, I heard a click and I turned slowly to see a creature only 10 meters away with a gun trained on my head.

"Drop your weapon, human." Though he said the words with ease his eyes darted around frantically. I could tell that he was nervous.

I saw his finger tense around the trigger and sensing a bullet coming, I dove onto the ground just as I heard the gun go off. I rolled over as the gun went off again. Only, this time, I felt searing pain burn through my shoulder. I grabbed another gun from a creature and went up on one knee firing twice at the creature that had shot me the first time. I watched as he slumped to the ground.

I got up shakily, looking around. There had been five creatures surrounding me. Now, all of them were dead. I slowly made my way around them. I looked up and saw the sun setting behind the horizon. It was bright but I made myself look at it. I made myself look at how far I had come. I made myself look at how far we had come. Now I knew that I was not going to give up now.

The sun was bright and it sparkled on the horizon. Its warmth was directed at me. It warmed me. It welcomed me. It embraced me. I fell to my knees. All this time I was still looking up at the sun. The sun was such a magical and powerful being. I felt my body relaxing. I felt my mind going numb. There was a voice calling me. The voice was soft, but powerful. I felt myself want to give in. I felt myself want to let go.

"You've got it. Get back on your feet, Caleb." A soft, but demanding, voice cut through my brain and I looked up from the ground. My father leaned over me. He had a stern, yet gentle, expression was on his face. He could have been handsome. His light blonde hair was cut short and his bright green eyes were piercing. His cheekbones were high on his face giving him a striking look. “Come on, Caleb,” my father urged, “you can do it.” He stuck his hand out toward me and I took it. He pulled me upwards and I was on my feet again.

“There is no time for you to quit now.” Then, he was gone. The sun and barren wasteland before me was back. I was on my feet again. I grasped the chain around my neck tightly, *do not let go.*

The sun disappeared behind the horizon and the cool air washed over me fast. I was ready to move on. What my father had told me all of my life was not to let go. He had told me not to let go of things that were important to me. But as I stared into the sun and watched it disappear behind the horizon I realized that it was time to finally figure out how to let go.

Justin was in the north side of the Resistance. There were many civilians gathered there but not even close to the amount that had been taking up the halls when I first came here. Some had injuries and were set up in the far corner of the room. Only around two hundred fighters were there and many of them were spaced out around the north side. They seemed to be keeping watch.

A doctor had approached me when I walked in and I let him clean my wound. It was not bad as the bullet had just skimmed me but the doctor insisted that it be cleaned none the less. The time that I was being cleaned seemed to drift by. Every second felt like a minute and every minute was an hour. I saw people coming and going. They walked in and out of the makeshift hospital, some cried but many stared straight ahead. They looked to be in shock.

This attack hurt them bad, I thought to myself, *they are not used to this type of devastation.*

A small girl helped one of the doctors by carrying out the equipment and trying to soothe the patients. Her height and small size said that she was far too young to be seeing anything like this. Experiencing it firsthand was even worse. The way she held her small body up when it looked like everything else was going to fall down, the way her jaw was set and tight in a straight line said otherwise.

Maybe there is hope for them. My thoughts were coming

slower now. I could feel the doctor's medicine kicking in. I could feel it working its way throughout my system. The medicine worked in a way similar to the creatures, it first falls in and sees what it has to conquer, then it will conquer, leaving only destruction in its wake. The thought made me sick, *does everything on this earth only move to conquer? Are we all greedy for revenge? Are we all greedy for our names to be remembered?*

The little girl that I saw before stood in front of me, "Are you okay, sir?" Her soft and smooth voice sounded like a lullaby and I smiled groggily.

"Yes, I am okay." My voice came out gruff but I didn't care. The little girl smiled too but the smile did not light up her face like it should.

"It's going to be okay, right?" Her voice and mind sought comfort. Comfort from wherever it could be found, even from me.

I drew her into a hug. It was a warm embrace that even soothed me. "Yes," I breathed out, "it will all be okay, I promise." I pulled away as the girl nodded. I saw some of the stress fade away from her face. Reassurance and hope is what matters. Reassurance and hope are what we all look for.

"I can't believe the creatures went out of their way to attack." Justin and I sat on the steps of the north side entrance. He was sporting a dark bruise on his upper cheek but nothing too terrible.

"I don't know. They must've felt threatened."

Justin shrugged, "I guess I didn't think they had it in them. I mean, I thought that they would sit back and watch us kill each other." I felt myself take a deep breath. That is exactly what General Daniels thought that the creatures would do. He did not believe that the creatures would attack. Justin sat back and rested his back against the wall. I made myself smile a little at what he said.

"Do you really believe that people are evil? Do you believe that the bugs are evil or is there a way to save them?" I asked the question. I was curious what Justin thought. Justin paused for a moment and I thought for a moment that he wouldn't answer. I thought about my question. Do the bugs even want to be saved?

Justin did answer. His voice was low when he spoke, "I think that there is always evil in people, in bugs and in creatures," he paused. I waited for him to say more, "In some people the good outweighs the evil… I think that we all need to be saved. We are all fighting battles on the inside. I believe that people as a whole are good but as individuals," he glanced at me and then continued, "we are not all that good." Justin stared straight ahead.

For the first time I wondered if he thought about dad the same as me. I wondered if he had the flashbacks. Justin closed his eyes and the thought escaped me. He can't. He does not act like it.

That's when I heard it, a little bit of static. "Troy," I breathed out. Justin opened his eyes, a look of bewilderment on his face. "Troy." I said again, I pointed to my ear. After all of this time I had forgotten about Troy, Troy at our base camp, Troy getting captured. What has happened to Troy now?

"I have to see if I can get a signal." I jumped up without waiting for his response and burst outside of the compound.

There were twelve of us. We were all standing in front of large wooden doors. I recognized no one, but that didn't mean anything. I had not been paying attention or trying to meet people. Finally, a man stepped forward. I recognized him at once. I recognized his dark skin and eyes, General Johnson.

He spoke, his voice glided smoothly throughout the chamber. I could tell that it filled everybody's ears with its sternness. "I have called all of you here to discuss battle plans and numbers. This will be the way that we will go about attacking the creatures. They made the first move, now it is our turn."

"Why is he here?" A man who looked in his mid twenties pointed at me from across the room, "he's too young. Shouldn't this meeting be with experienced people only?" His voice was strong.

I could tell that he was very confident in himself. He looked cocky. A disgusted feeling took place in my stomach as he spoke and I wanted to punch the man in the face. The general took two long strides forward. He grabbed the man's shirt and pulled him up off of the ground. General Johnson spoke in a low voice but it carried over to us all.

"He is a far more skilled fighter and thinker than you, Jefferson. So, if you want to be here in this meeting you better shut up." I saw Jefferson's Adam's apple bob up and down a few times before he gulped and then nodded his head.

Without another word the general turned on his heels and walked away. He walked through the wooden doors into the room. The people who had been called to the meeting all started whispering to each other, pointing at me and giving me looks that made me believe that I did not belong.

My eyes fell upon Jefferson. He gave me a look of pure hatred before slipping into the room after the general. The rest of the group followed close behind.

Everyone had gathered around a table when I entered the room. The general was standing nearest to it. He was pointing at something. I walked closer to try and get a good view but there were so many people that I could not see well. Slowly, I made my way closer to the general and could hear some words that he said, "This is where…most are covered here… we will attack in groups… some will take the closest…" Finally, I got to where I could see the table and hear what the general was saying.

It was a map that displayed the creature's base. The map showed where the groups of fighters would enter and where they would retreat if necessary. It showed the numbers of the creature's compound. Above the table was a clock. The clock showed: 8:38:24. I breathed a deep sigh, Eight days until we attack the creatures. Eight days to prepare all troops. Eight days to make everyone aware and ready for battle. Eight days until…

Then I saw a problem with his plan, "Sir," I weakly raised my hand. I was unsure how he reacted to interruptions. He continued talking. He was either ignoring me or he did not hear me. I cleared my throat, and spoke louder, sure that there was a problem, "Sir." My voice was strong, much unlike the feeling inside me.

The general stopped talking and looked at me. It was a look that pierced into my soul. I shivered. "Yes, Mr. Hanson?" His voice was almost mocking, "What do you want, because I know that you probably-"

I interrupted him again, "How are we going to get out?"

He gave a short laugh and looked around himself as if my question was stupid. He looked back at me and then at the map and pointed to one of the groups, "See these will go in and exit through the sewer system, it's almost never guarded and if it is explosives will do the job-"

"And risk collapsing the rest of the building?" I shook my head as I stepped closer to the map. The general pursed his lips as I continued, "Okay," I was getting more sure of myself now, "say the building miraculously doesn't collapse, and that group gets out fine, what about this group?" I gestured to the map at a group that would have gone in before the group exiting through the sewers, "you leave this group no option to escape," I paused, "they are trapped."

The general was furious now he walked up to me and put his face close to mine, "What are you suggesting Hanson?" His dark skin gleamed and his black eyes rippled with anger.

"I suggest that you put this group," I gestured to the group that would have been trapped, "in through the sewer system, if it's rarely guarded then that would be a perfect place to attack. I suggest that you have this group be guarded by the groups entering around them. This is the group that should hit them hard." I gestured to a group that would be surrounded by reinforcements.

"And where is that?" His anger was increasing as I spoke and his voice was laced with vehemence.

"Well their leader of course."

"Their leader?"

"Yes."

The look of hatred on the general's face quickly turned into one of embarrassment. The general eyed the map then turned to the left, to a control panel. He quickly pushed some buttons and then turned back to the map.

Everything that I suggested appeared on the map. The general stared. Slowly, whispers started up through the crowd. The whispers were quiet at first, but then they grew louder and louder until some people were even shouting.

I stood staring at the general he watched as the scene played out. All of the groups got out of the creature's base safely.

The general looked up and met my gaze. His eyes now showed something other than hatred and embarrassment. His eyes showed something that I wanted from people older than me for a long time. His eyes showed respect. He nodded at me and I nodded back.

I was going to fight.

I shook my head slowly from side to side barely believing what I felt around me. Men and women, surrounding me, we all had the same goal, to save the world.

There's that word again, save. Is saving my destiny?

That's what it is, when man has a common goal they work together, but as our goals begin to change, to stray away from the goal, that's when man gets wrong. I have to believe that the creatures and bugs are the same, they believe in the common goal.

But they still can be saved.

I looked up at everyone surrounding me, we were going to fight. We were going to fight and win, it could be done.

My eyes found someone on the other side of the room. She turned and her golden hair flung over her shoulder, her blue eyes found mine and pierced through me, deep inside. I saw a smile light up her face. Slowly, I began to make my way over to her.

"Hey," I breathed out when I reached her.

"Hey," she smiled back at me and I felt my heart leap up in my chest.

I stood there for a moment. I was unsure of what to do. "Can we talk for a little?" I asked Jami. I gestured towards the door.

"Sure," she started making her way towards the doorway, her hair swung back as she turned, so effortlessly, but not as carefree as before.

"Are you okay?" We had walked outside of the room and into a lightened corridor. It was not bright light but I could see her well. Her face was beautiful illuminated by the light. There was one thing missing, her smile.

"Yeah..." She answered breathing out slowly. Her sharp blue eyes found my green ones. She stared for a long moment. It was me that looked away first, "I guess that I just want revenge now." She shrugged, gazing off into the distance.

"I know what you mean…" Suddenly I had the urge to comfort her. Her light eyebrows were furrowed together in worry making her look even more beautiful than before.

I reached out and softly grabbed her hand. She was hesitant at first and I thought that she was going to pull away.

She took a step towards me. I linked my fingers through hers. Then, she took another step and then another. I closed the distance between us and pulled her into a hug.

Her grip was strong. Finally she pulled away. Her blue eyes gazed up at me. They were bright again, full of the glow that I loved.

"Caleb?" She asked. Her eyebrows furrowed together again.

"Yes?" I asked.

"What happened to you in the southwest side of the Resistance? I mean, Justin came back with a family and some others but you weren't with him."

"I ran into some creatures," I decided not to elaborate. Instead, I glanced down the corridor. "What about you?"

She hesitated. I guessed that she was unsure how much to tell me. "Tell me as much as you want." I hoped that my face was open. Jami nodded her head.

"General Johnson insisted that I stay with him. He decided that we should secure the perimeter, or as much of it that we had left. We walked around. It seemed like the general was looking for something, or someone, I don't know why, he doesn't have a wife or kids, or even parents. He came to the Resistance a year before me. He came here alone." She stopped and looked at me.

"Why did you come here?" I asked the question out of curiosity. However, there was an edge to my voice that I did not intend to be there.

"It's okay, really." Jami reached out and touched my arm sending waves of electricity coursing through my body. "I was curious, about the Resistance I mean. They were always so controlling and I wanted to know why, I wanted to know their secret. I never did trust General Daniels, he always seemed…" She trailed off, and then glanced up at me.

“Greedy?” I asked. My jaw was set in a straight line my voice came out sharp. Jami nodded. I took a deep breath and then ran my hand through my hair.

Jami continued, “Well, I was caught by the officers. They banished me from the Resistance.”

“They banished you just like that?” I asked softly. “I mean, you weren’t even really doing anything.”

Jami nodded, “Just like that.”

I felt another surge of anger towards the Resistance, anger towards the place that always felt like home to me. Anger towards the place where I thought I belonged, the place that I trusted to do the right thing.

“Did you find it? What you were looking for?”

Jami looked up at me, an expression on her face that I had not seen before, was it fear, or was it anger, or was it something else entirely?

Her blue eyes shone bright, and the light gleamed off of her hair. Standing there in the hallway she was so beautiful.

I felt myself leaning in towards her. Her body was like a magnet. Jami leaned in at the same time as me. I touched her chin slightly and she shivered. I tilted it to the side as our bodies slid in beside each other.

Right before our lips met, Jami breathed out a word, “Yes.” She said softly. She continued forward, her lips right about to meet mine, “I did find what I was looking for.”

That is all I remember before our lips met and energy coursed through my body. We melted into each other. As we kissed we became one.

CHAPTER 12

Justin was in his room. He was reading a book and turned the page as I walked in. Justin looked up.

"Well hello, Cheery." Justin smiled as he spoke watching me practically skip into his room.

I felt myself laugh. My insides felt light and I felt happy for the first time in months. I felt as light as a feather.

"Did you get a signal from Troy?" Suddenly, my happy feeling dropped. I felt my smile slide of my face. "Well, I didn't want to kill your mood, sorry."

Justin held up his hands in a look of surrender. It was such a childish move that I felt a smile start to creep back up onto my face.

I stepped forward and sat at the foot of his bed. "No, it's okay." I sighed and ran my hand through my hair, a habit that I couldn't get rid of. "I was not able to get a signal from Troy. I hope that he's okay."

"I'm sure that he's fine." Justin spoke with such reassurance that I almost believed him but hearing Jami's story about being banished by doing practically nothing, I was not so sure. "So you couldn't contact him?" Justin asked the question again, as if he didn't believe what I said the first time. I shook my head.

"No, I feel like I was close but it didn't even sound like it was Troy trying to speak to me."

"Do you think that the general captured him again? I mean, you told me that you contacted him in the creature's arena."

"Yeah, I was able to contact him in the arena. I don't

know. I haven't been able to contact him since."

"That's interesting, how was he able to contact you in the first place? I thought that you turned your receiver off." I had turned my receiver off. I ran my hand through my hair. My mind was racing.

"Do you think that there is some sort of back up mode, so that he could contact me whenever he wanted?"

Justin shrugged, "I didn't think of that." He paused for a moment, "Why were you in such a good mood anyways?"

I hesitated, remembering Jami, remembering her soft lips and bright blue eyes that sparkled when she was excited. I felt my stomach drop as I listened to myself speak. "We created the battle plan. We will attack the creatures in about eight days from now." That was true. It was not a lie but I still winced speaking out the words.

Justin sat up in his bed, "Really? The general created an attack on the creatures?" Justin leaned back, resting his back against his headboard, "Wow."

"Why is this so shocking too you?" I asked. I wanted to be able to tell Justin the whole truth.

Justin looked up at me. His dark brown eyes met mine. He was handsome. The way his light brown hair was naturally messy was handsome. The way he moved with such confidence was handsome as well. So why did Jami like me and not him? What did she see in me?

"After the battle the general looked so defeated that I thought he would give up right then and there." Justin paused, staring off into the distance. "It looked like someone had gone through and ripped his heart out of his chest. It looked like he was just going to lie down and stop doing anything." Justin shook his head, remembering.

He must not have found what he was looking for, I thought. I remembered what Jami had told me about him trying to find something as they both worked to secure the perimeter. I remembered everything she had said.

"Well I guess he decided to step up and attack. I didn't think that he had it in him." Justin was looking at me closely. It was as if he could tell that I was holding back some part of the truth.

I forced a smile, "Well, we get to fight."

Justin nodded. Suddenly, Justin stood. He walked quickly over to his dresser and pulled out a piece of paper from inside one of the top drawers. He looked at it and then handed it to me.

Before I looked at the paper, Justin spoke, "I brought this all the way from home. I couldn't leave it behind."

I looked down at the paper and saw a picture.

I was sitting on my father's shoulders. I was no more than five. Justin was standing in front of our father. He was laughing at what our father had just said. Dad was laughing too. The laughter lit up his face.

I remembered back to that day. The air smelled sweet like grass and rain. It was a family outing. Even mom was there. Her hair was down. It was flowing over her shoulders. Dad was laughing as were Justin and I. The sun was shining bright and birds chirped loudly. The birds were singing beautifully in tune with our laughter.

I looked up. Justin was looking at me. There was a look of amusement on his face, but there was something else there too, "Another flashback?"

I nodded.

Justin nodded too. All of a sudden Justin pulled me close into a hug. "It's going to be alright," he whispered softly into my ear, "It's going to be… alright."

At that moment, everything else that I had been worrying about disappeared. At that moment, I felt grateful. Grateful that Justin, my brother, was there.

I needed air. Fresh air. I tore through the tunnels of the Resistance. It was underground and I was beginning to lose my mind from being underground for so long. I could feel my body calling out for fresh air.

Finally, I found steps leading up. A door at the top of the steps was marked exit. I flung it open and bolted outside. The cool night air washed over me and I immediately started to relax. It was like air from the outdoors was my relief, my exhale, my haven.

I found a spot in the grass and laid down. The grass was soft to the touch and cold. I felt awake. I felt alive. I felt free. My heart raced, but I was alive. I was outside and I could accomplish anything.

I looked up at the stars. There was not much pollution here. I could see a lot of stars clearly and brightly. I sighed. Now I could feel my breath come and go easier. I could feel the outdoors stretch around me in every direction. I could hear the coo of the night owl and could smell the scent of soft rain in the distance. I felt home, but most of all, I felt alive. I finally felt saved.

The battle. It was in seven days from now and I felt ready. The time clawed at me. The time was trying to make me give in to the pressure of it but I stood strong. I would keep standing strong until the battle was over.

Seven more days, then we will avenge my father. For some reason, that did not get me anxious again. Avenging my father did not have that same light that it had before. Avenging my father did not make me want to leave now and fight the creatures on my own. Avenging my father felt dull, like a reason that was used too much and now did not hold the same edge that it used to.

No, in seven days from now, we will save the world.

I could hear the chirping of crickets, the soft howl of the wind as it blew past and ruffled my hair, and the steady beating of my heart, calm now. I could feel the soft caress of the grass against my skin and the cool night air on my face. I could tell that I was ready for battle. I was ready to fight. I was ready to fight for what I loved.

"Caleb?" The voice was soft but I could recognize it anywhere. I did not answer at first. I wanted to hear her voice again. "Caleb?" She asked, a little louder now. I could feel her turn. I could hear her start to leave.

"Don't go." I said softly hoping the wind would carry my voice to her ears as it carried hers to mine.

She stopped and turned around. I heard her make her way back to me and lay on the ground beside me. She was warm. I reached out and touched her hand, it was soft in mine. Our fingers intertwined, we were meant to be.

"It is so peaceful out here." Jami's soft voice drifted into my ears.

"I know," I said softly. I breathed out. I wanted to capture this moment forever and just lie here with Jami. "I love it out here."

Her heart was beating in the same rhythm as mine. I leaned over to her and kissed her cheek. I heard her heartbeat quicken as I did so.

I smiled. She curled up against me. Her body was soft and fit into me perfectly.

"Can we just lie here and forget about the rest of the world? Please? Just you and me?" I asked softly.

I heard her gasp softly under her breath. I immediately regretted the question, of course we couldn't. The thought of me and Jami together, forever, it was tempting, but it wouldn't work. Instead of waiting for her to answer I leaned over and kissed her. She was kissing me back. She was kissing me back hard.

I held her close. I wanted all the space and distance between us to disappear. I wanted us to be together with nothing to stand in our way.

Justin.

I stopped and leaned back down to the ground. Jami leaned back too. "We can't." Jami said simply.

"I know." I pulled her to me again and held her tight. Her hands curled around me and looped over my waist.

"Maybe after, after this all clears up…" She spoke with hopeful eagerness in her voice but I could hear the hint of doubt that she tried to hide, the doubt in her voice that would always be there, the doubt hidden in her voice that was waiting for the right moment to pounce.

"I understand." I spoke softly, as to not ruin the moment.

Jami leaned over again and we kissed. At that moment the whole world melted away and it was just me and Jami.

"My name is Caleb. I will be your leader for this mission." I looked at each and every one of my troops making eye contact with each of them. I needed them all to know that they belonged. "Troops line up. You all know that we do not have much time here. The battle is only seven days from now and we have a lot to learn. However, I am confident that we will get our training done in time for the battle. This training will not be easy. It will be difficult but I want each and every one of you to fight through the pain. That is what makes good fighters. Warriors, warriors are people that outlast everyone else and are the last ones left standing.

"First we will start with one-on-one combat.

"Each and every one of you will be able to take everyone else down by the time we are done here. I will pair you up first based on size, but even the smallest of us will be able to fight and win against the biggest.

"You," I gestured at one of the bigger troops, "What is your name?"

"Nick," he answered. His voice was low.

"Nick, you will start off fighting Ben." I motioned for Ben, the largest of the group to step forward.

Nick nodded and went off to stand by Ben.

I went down the line. I picked out evenly sized fighters to start off. There were eight troops. Eight troops to work with to bring the creatures down, eight troops that had little experience and not much time.

"You will all start off fighting on my signal. First, it is hand-to hand. Then, we will move up to weapons.

"Go!" I yelled. On my command all of the groups started fighting.

I began to walk around. I corrected some groups. I told them words of praise when they listened and corrected to what I had said.

Finally, I got to Nick and Ben. Ben was slow but Nick was not much faster. Nick did not use his size. Instead, he stayed low to the ground. He was always ready to move. I was impressed by how much he already knew.

Ben was the opposite. He stood straight up and had his hands out in front of himself cupped into fists. Nick lunged at Ben and Ben swung a punch. He missed and Nick hit him hard in the gut.

Ben grunted but grabbed Nick's arm and shoved him back. Nick stumbled and fell. Ben advanced and kicked Nick in the stomach.

"Stop," I said. It was a command but Ben did not listen. He drew his leg back again. Ready to kick, "I said, stop." I spoke in a hard commanding voice. Ben kicked again.

I lunged forward and punched Ben hard in the side of the

head. He fell to the ground. All of the other groups had stopped fighting. They were watching what I would do. I lifted Ben back up with one hand and punched him in the stomach with the other.

Then, I let him fall hard to the ground. "You obey my commands." I said softly turning to my troops, "I am your leader, and you will all listen to what I say."

The other troops nodded, fear was on their faces. "Now get back to work."

The troops ran quickly back to their stations. They began fighting with more vigor and intensity than before.

"Sir?" I turned to see Nick standing behind me.

"Yes?"

"Sir, you didn't have to do that for me. I can take a hit. I could have gotten back up onto my feet." Nick's eyebrows furrowed together.

"I did not do that for you, Nick. I did that so that everyone would know that I was in charge. I did that so that people would listen to my commands because, in battle, it gets… scary."

Nick nodded but he still did not look at ease.

"What's the matter?" I asked. I heard the sympathy creep into my voice. Nick looked up at me. His brown eyes were so dark.

"It's just. I've never been in a battle before. This is the first time for me to be fighting."

"Hey, don't worry about it," but as Nick said those words I myself began to worry. Had everyone in my group not fought before? "You believe in this battle, right?"

Nick nodded his head up and down.

"Then you will be fine, as long as your heart is in it."

Nick nodded, he believed me. I began to believe myself.

"Don't worry," I said to Nick, "by the time the battle comes I will have you all ready, I promise."

Nick smiled, "Yes, Sir."

I started walking back around to the other groups. There was definitely some work to be done.

"Now we will be working on uppercuts." I spoke to the group. I could see the sweat dripping from their bodies. Good, I thought to myself, they are all working hard. "Now, I want you all to put in as much strength as you can into each hit. It will hurt and you will be tired but you all will appreciate it in the end."

Eli, the shortest kid with long hair that hung into his eyes groaned. I stared at him hard.

"Alright then, Eli, you can come and demonstrate." I motioned for Eli to step forward. He looked around at everyone else. Hoping there was some way out. "Come on, Eli, it's all you." I stepped back from the bag. He looked at me but after seeing what I did to Ben he did as he was told.

He stepped up to the bag that was filled with sand. "Go on. Hit it like I told you."

Eli looked at the bag. Then, without bending his knees or getting into a fighting stance he threw his fist back and swung forward. I did not cringe like the troops did when I heard his fist hit the bag though it made a large cracking sound.

"Ow," Eli cried out in pain and clutched his hand.

"Again," I said. Eli looked at me, incredulous, and did not move to the bag. I waited for a moment then spoke. "I said, again."

Eli grimaced, and looked back at the bag. He did the same as before, he slung his hand back and sent it flailing forwards at the bag. It contacted again and Eli immediately pulled his hand away, cradling it to his chest.

"Again," I spoke low but loud enough for all of the troops to hear. Eli didn't even turn away from the bag. Instead he flung his fist forward as hard as he could.

I lunged forward and caught his fist right before it hit the bag.

"You should not hit like that unless you want to break your hand. Get into your fighting stance." Eli looked back at the group. Someone must have made a face because Eli smiled. I swung my leg back and kicked his knees out from under him. Eli hit the floor hard. His back smacked onto the ground. Eli rolled over, groaning. "Get up." I told him. Eli didn't move, "I said get up."

Eli rolled to his feet and stood, hunched over. "That would not have happened if you would have been in your stance.

"Get into your stance." This time Eli obeyed.

He got low, bending his knees slightly, but not enough, "Lower," I told him, he listened again, "You are small," I told him,

"Use that to your advantage. Create an even lower center of gravity for yourself and you will be quicker than any creature."

"So creatures are real?" One of the troops asked.

I stared at the group. It was Phillip that asked the question. He had dark hair that hung just below his eyebrows. His eyes were like the sea, and were a majestic blue. Like Jami's. Jami.

"Yes." I answered firmly, "the creatures are real and they are quick. You cannot outrun them. The only way to defeat them is to stand your ground and fight."

I turned back to Eli. "Dismissed," I told him. Eli scampered into the back of the group.

"Go and practice." I said to the group, "two people per sandbag. Try to correct the other person."

Finally, the day was over. Six, more to go, I thought to myself. This was going to be a long week.

As I was packing up my bags I heard a noise behind me. I turned around and saw Phillip standing there. I looked into his eyes again. They were just like Jami's.

"Phillip," I said nodding at him, "What's up?"

Phillip paused and took an intake of breath, "I am very nervous about the battle, Sir. I really do not know what to expect. I had no idea that creatures were real. My sister always said that they were but I did not believe her."

I put my hand on his shoulder, his eyes looked scared. "It's going to be okay, Phillip." He looked up at me.

"But, Sir."

"Phillip, do you believe in what you are fighting for?"

He nodded.

"Good," I said, "that way everything will fall into place."

"Thank you, Sir." He turned away to leave.

"Phillip? Who is your sister?"

He turned back to me, his eyebrows furrowed, "Jami Kearns." He said.

I felt myself breathe in softly through my nose. Then, I nodded. He was Jami's sister.

"You may go, Phillip." He nodded, and then left.

I sat down. How was he Jami's brother? How did he get

in my group? I shook my thoughts away. I could not let anything happen to him. I would not let anything happen to him.

That night, I met with Jami. I felt the need to talk to her, to be with her, and to hold her tight. It felt like the last time that we really would be able to hold each other like nothing else mattered. It felt like the last time that we would be able to touch freely without feelings for anything else.

"Only six more days," I whispered in her ear, "then we will be fighting again for what we love."

"I already am," she whispered back.

We kissed. I felt electricity shoot though my body. She was beautiful. I felt her smooth hair on my fingertips. It was so soft.

I pulled away for a moment. "I met your brother today." I told her.

She laughed, "He's annoying, huh?"

I laughed. I felt free when I was with Jami, I felt light and happy. I felt full of life. Jami was so sweet, "He does ask a lot of questions. He asked me today if creatures were really real. He told me that he never believed you." I paused. "He is in my group." I told her, suddenly, I was serious.

"Hey, it's okay," she whispered softly, "I know that you won't let anything happen to him. I trust you Caleb."

With that she kissed me again. This time, we kissed hard as if we really were already fighting for what and who we loved. I felt like everything else, all of my problems and worries seemed to melt away.

I quickly learned that Nick was turning out to be the best fighter. We only had three days left before the battle, but I felt that my troops were close. They were almost ready.

I had seen a lot of improvement over the course of the week. Each of my troops picked their favorite weapon. This weapon would be the one that they would use in the battle. Nick chose the double sided axe and I did not stop him. He was great with it.

"The battle is in three days." I spoke to my troops. They all cheered. "I believe that we are ready. Tomorrow, we will practice again but the last day I will give you guys off. Spend time with your families and enjoy that day. The next day, we will fight for our families. We will fight to save the world." The troops cheered again.

I could tell now that we were a family. We would do anything for each other. We were a team. I smiled. We could fight to save the world. We could save the world because we were all prepared. We were all ready and we all wanted to beat the creatures. They would not win this war.

CHAPTER 13

"All troops report to your leaders. All troops report to your leaders immediately. Be prepared for combat."

I took a deep breath as I waited for my troops. The day was here. It was finally time to fight. I was wearing the black suit that Troy had equipped for me the first day, the first day that we had set off on the mission.

The day seemed so long ago now. It had been so long since the beginning. It had been so long since I had seen Grandfather. I felt the heartache for home. I felt myself want to go back. First things first, I thought to myself, first, the fight.

I was ready. I was ready to fight for what I loved.

"Attention troops. It is time to fight." I spoke in a commanding voice and my troops cheered. I caught Nick's eye and nodded at him. His face was pale white but he smiled and cheered along with the other troops. He had gotten considerably better by the end of my seven days with him and could beat all of the troops easily now. Nick leaned over to Eli and whispered something in his ear. Eli smiled and laughed. He looked up at me and nodded. A sign of respect and courage, Eli was ready for battle, too.

We boarded our craft and it took off into the sky. I counted the troops, eight. My heartbeat quickened. Every second we were getting closer and closer to reaching our goal. Every second I was getting closer and closer to reaching my goal.

I looked out the window of the craft. The sky was black and only a few stars were out. There was no moon.

My troops were nervous. I could tell by the ways they fidgeted with their weapons, the way their breathing was unsteady, and the way their eyes darted around every time the craft hit a bump. Nick's face had returned to a normal color as had Eli's, they tried to comfort the other troops. I could tell that Ben was the most nervous of all. He had his arm draped carelessly over his gun. His foot bounced up and down slightly. But, every time we hit a bump Ben would cringe and look around. His face would turn a pale white.

"It's going to be okay," I heard myself say, "We have the element of surprise, remember that." Seeing some of my troops nod I turned back to the window.

I was going to be okay. We could defeat the creatures. There was no turning back now.

I stared at the trees that we passed. There were so few of them that it looked like a wasteland.

"There used to be forests." I heard my father say, "They were huge and stretched across huge areas and regions."

"What's a forest?" I was young, no more than seven.

My father sighed. "Life," he answered. When he did not elaborate I asked.

"What type of life?" Father looked at me an expression on his face that I had seen before, an expression like something had been taken away from me.

Father went on to describe a forest, the life and trees, so many trees. I was impressed and in awe. But when I asked father what happened to the forest father just shook his head.

"We destroyed the forests. Mankind wiped them out. We realized what we were doing eventually but it was too late. That is when the radiation hit. Mankind fell. I have a feeling that we are not the rulers of Earth anymore. Now we live in fear of the creatures of the forest, the bugs but most of all, the beasts."

I nodded, even though I didn't truly understand what he was saying. I did not truly understand until days later when my father pointed out a tree to me. It was the first tree I had ever seen and it was dying.

"Can't we save it?" I asked softly to my father. He nodded and from that day on I watered the tree and took care of it. It grew and thrived.

I think that everything and everyone is waiting to be saved. Saved. We only have to find the courage and the strength to save them.

I opened my eyes, the craft was still flying but I could see the changes in scenery. We were close.

I looked around at my troops, none of them spoke. Not even Ian said anything. He stared ahead and closed his eyes.

"We are close." I told them, and saw many of them get tense as I spoke. Ian opened his eyes and looked at me. I smiled at him, but it came out more like a grimace. I looked down at the blinking red light on the wrist of my suit. I marked where we were and where we had to jump. "1 minute to the jump."

I stood and walked over to the door of the craft. Slipping my face mask over my face I saw my troops do the same. "30 seconds." I pushed a button on the side of the door and heard the metal creak as the latch opened. Below us everything was rushing by so fast.

Above the door a timer was started, it was blinking down the seconds. 15… I closed my eyes, when I opened them I looked around and all of my troops were standing beside me ready to jump. 10…9…8… "Prepare for jump!" I yelled over the howling wind, 5…4…3…2…1, "Now!" I yelled and hopped out of the craft into the dark night.

I spread out my arms and legs and coasted to a stop by the back of the creature's base. I heard my troops land softly behind me. We started forward at a quick place.

On the wrist of my suit I could see the other groups that were surrounding ours. We were the queen bee, the one that was going to hit the creatures where would it hurt. We were going to take out the creatures' leader.

On either side of my group there was another group. Three separate groups entered through the north side of the base.

Finally, I saw the sewer system and motioned for my troops to enter. I had not seen any movement so far. When Nick was about to enter I held him back, "I want you to stay at the back of the group," I told him, "you are our strongest fighter and we need you to protect our back." Nick nodded his head and clutched his weapon.

I started forward when Nick grabbed my arm, “Be careful, okay, Caleb?”

“Sure,” I told him. Nick nodded again and then stepped back to let the other troops pass, I continued onward.

It was dark and damp in the sewer. The tunnel was so dark that I could barely make out the shape of my hand when I held it in front of my face. My group stuck to one side, careful to avoid the stream of water flowing through the center. My suit started to blink red, “Poisonous gasses, poisonous gases.” My suit said in my ear.

“Poisonous gases are ahead.” I said through the microphone in my helmet, “Turn your oxygen on.” I instructed my team.

We continued onward. I held my cutlass tightly in my hand, the double-sided blade out and ready for battle. My eyes had finally adjusted to the darkness. I could now make out shapes, but the lighting was still too dark to see clearly. We continued another 20 feet before I felt something.

Suddenly, I heard a high-pitched, blood-curdling cry. The beast had a weapon of noise.

One of my troops, Phillip I think, yelled and covered his ears with his hands. I heard hard breathing through my helmet.

“What was that?” Nick asked softly, his low voice cut easily through the night. I could hear the fear in his voice.

“I don’t know.” One of the troops responded, I could not place his voice. I could hear my troops gripping their weapons tightly.

“It was a beast,” I spoke calmly, “they guard the creatures and will protect and defend them at all costs, we must be ready for battle,” I said, hoping my voice was calm. I needed my troops to be mentally in this fight, otherwise…

My troops took an intake of breath but continued onward with me.

I felt a shift in the air, the presence of a beast.

I held up my hand, stopping my troops from advancing. “The beast is close.” I spoke slowly and softly, not wanting to startle the beast if it could sense vibrations of noise. “Ready your weapons."

Suddenly, I saw movement, a shadow, on the other side of the sewer system. "Movement to the left, there has been movement to the left." I spoke calmly into my microphone. I needed my troops to relax.

"You must learn to calm your fear, Caleb. Nerves? Those are fine but fear is what will destroy you. It is what destroyed mankind." My father's voice echoed in my head.

"Relax," I told my troops, "We can defeat the beast, we will work together."

Suddenly I saw the shadow move quickly. It leapt forward and I tensed, ready for battle. All I saw was teeth as long as my arms bearing down at me before I was knocked to the ground.

The beast screamed again, and I heard my troops yell. I hopped to my feet. The beast had taken out one of my eight troops. "Regroup," I ordered, "Regroup." My troops spun around, Nick was facing the beast now, trying to hold it off.

I leapt forward with my cutlass in hand and sunk the blade of my cutlass through the beast's skull. It whimpered and then fell to the ground. My eyes made contact with Nick's I gave him a nod but there was no time for praise.

"Someone, help Ian." I instructed, pointing at my troop that was struggling to get up, "He will be okay." Ben stooped down to help Ian up.

"Come on," I told them, "We have to move, before more of them come."

I started forward, continuing down the sewer. There was no time to stop. We were so close and I did not want to signal any of the alarms.

"Take next right," my suit instructed. I looked back at my troops, they looked scared. I saw Nick swallow hard. I could tell that he was the most ready of all of the troops for battle. He was the most mentally prepared and I knew that our mental strength would win us this battle. Our mental strength would save the world.

"We can do this, we are all good fighters. Beasts can be taken down easily if we work together." I said, trying to sound reassuring. "We will be entering the base of the creatures now. It is time to be on the lookout. Remember our goal, find the leader." I knew that I was being harsh but there was no time to stop. We had to continue forward. We had to complete our part of the plan, otherwise everything would be lost.

The creature's base was exactly as I remembered it. The halls were long and made of metal. It sounded like our footsteps echoed throughout the whole base. Sharp turns went off in every direction. I took a deep breath. It would be so easy to get lost in here.

"Keep close," I warned my troops, "make sure you stay together."

The hallways were empty, much like they were when the creatures brought me to the arena. They know that we are here, I thought to myself.

"Where is everyone?" I heard Eli ask.

"They know that we are here." I heard Nick respond. His voice was calm and steady but the way he breathed I could tell that he was nervous.

"I don't know if they do… The hallways are always this empty." I spoke softly, "Be ready for anything." I told my troops, "They could be anywhere."

I saw Eli nod out of the corner of my eye and draw closer to me.

He is young. I thought to myself, I can't lose him in here.

The metallic hallway abruptly ended and my group and I emerged into a dirt tunnel. The light was dim but I could see brightness up ahead.

The sun, I thought to myself.

"What is that?" I heard Phillip ask softly.

I heard screaming and shouts, clashing of metal and firing of guns.

"This is it." I heard Nick answer Phillip softly. "This is the final battle."

CHAPTER 14

We were almost out of the tunnel. I was mentally preparing myself for battle. I held onto my cutlass tight.

"We can do this," I told my team, "stick together and no one will be able to get around us."

Without warning I felt a sword press against my throat. I heard Eli give out a yelp.

Laughter filled the air as five creatures stepped out from seemingly nowhere to block our path to the fight.

I could hear the creatures move with their unnatural speed behind us too, to block our exit.

My eyes focused on the creature with the blade at my throat.

"Leader of the humans…" The creature's teasing voice filled the cave, "I thought that you would be more careful."

I ignored the creature and instead spoke to my troops, "Do not lose hope," I spoke to them, slowly and calmly, "there is always a way, I promise."

I could see Nick straighten out of the corner of my eye, he understood. I breathed a sigh of relief.

I smiled at the creature, "Well, we humans like to be in the right place at the right time."

I did not wait to see the creatures puzzled look, instead I opened my cutlass and in one sharp move drove it forward into the creature's stomach.

Nick moved at the same time as me, his double-sided axe flew through the air and I saw it lodge into one of the creatures nearest to me.

I pulled my cutlass out of the creature and spun around taking out two with one strike. By now the rest of my troops had acted. I saw Eli impale a creature. He turned and smiled at me, I smiled back right as I heard Nick yell, "Duck!" He screamed. I dropped to the ground as one of Nick's double-sided axes flew over my head. I looked up and saw the axe impale a creature's head. The creature had a sword in hand. He looked like he was about to bring it down. Nick threw his axe into his other hand and nodded at me.

"Be careful, Sir." His smooth voice cut through the night. Nick grabbed his axe from out of the creature and hoisted it to his shoulder.

I looked around. The ten creatures that had ambushed us were dead. We had done it. We had won our first battle.

"Sir?" It was Eli. He was kneeling on the ground beside Ben.

I raced over to where he was and took a deep breath, looking into Ben's eyes. They were blank, staring off into the distance. Into some far away land that no one else knew about.

"No," I whispered softly, "No!" I yelled, getting to my feet. I stormed to the cave wall and clutched it tight. I clutched it until my hands started turning white.

"He saved me," Eli whimpered, "if it wouldn't have been for me he wouldn't be…" Silent tears raced down Eli's cheeks.

"Oh no, Eli," I reached down and pulled Eli into an embrace, "Eli, it was not your fault at all. Eli, I need you to look at me." Eli's tear-streaked face glanced up. His eyes were sad, full of sorrow. "Eli, it was not your fault. I need you to understand that." Eli looked away, "Eli."

He nodded his head, up and down, once.

Hearing the battle cries rise up again and find their way into the cave, I looked around. Each boy had tears streaking their faces. Each boy looked so young. Each boy was determined to win this battle. Each boy was not going to let anything stand in their way.

"Now we must fight. We are needed in battle. Remember the mission. Find the leader. For Ben!" I screamed.

"For Ben!" All of my troops screamed back. With that I turned and sprinted with all of my strength to the opening of the tunnel. With that I turned my back on what had just happened there. With that final yell we were entering a situation which would probably cause death. With that yell we were finally facing our fears, but most of all, our dreams. With that final yell, we would finally do what we came to do: save the world.

I did not think when we first entered the battle. I just acted. Creatures were everywhere, they were pouring out of caves from all over. I could see the men dropping.

I looked up, scanning the mass. At first I did not know what I was looking for but I finally found him, well, it. The leader. He was being ushered by at least ten creatures out of the battle field. He was getting away.

I found Nick's eyes. He knew what I wanted.

"I will follow you." I could hear his voice cut through the battle cries. I could hear his voice cut through the death and destruction. I could hear his voice through my heart which was now pounding in my throat.

"I'm coming too." I turned and saw Eli pull his sword out from one of the creatures. He stepped back, realizing that I would protest, "you can't stop me." He said fiercely, "you need me and I know it. I'm coming." He said again. There was such fierceness in his eyes that I did not argue. He was right, we would need him.

With that I turned and started making my way back through the battle.

Gradually we made our way through the battle. I knew now that our only chance would be to take out the leader, otherwise men would fall. Mankind would be… lost.

The tunnel that we entered was white, a marble type of material.

"What is this place?" Eli asked, "It's not like the other tunnels at all."

"I know," I breathed out. I was astonished by the architecture of this whole building, how it all connects and was laid out with such care and effort.

As we continued to walk down the hallway, slowly and cautiously we did not speak. I could hear Nick's breathing though. It was loud in the marble tunnel. It sounded thick.

We did not see where the creatures had gone but there were no forks in the tunnel. There were no choices in where to go. There was only straight ahead, straight ahead with no ways to escape, straight ahead with only one way to the leader.

"Are you sure that they came this way?" I heard Eli ask softly, "I mean, don't you think that it would be stupid to go into one of the only tunnels without separate paths? Don't you think that they would know they were being followed?"

The sound of lost confidence in his voice made me second guess myself. What if I had chosen the wrong pathway? What if my eyes were playing tricks on me and I had just believed that the creatures had gone this way? What if I was leading us to a dead end?

I instinctively turned around, feeling eyes on the back of my head. All I saw was more of the marble tunnel, more of where we had just come from, but no creatures.

"I don't know," I heard myself answer Eli. I could hear the doubt in my own voice, "I think that the creatures went this way but I am not so sure anymore."

I took a deep breath and continued onward, more and more into the white and spotless tunnel.

We walked in silence for another five minutes. Well, it felt like five minutes, but time seemed to drag on in the tunnel, I was not sure how long it had been since we had left the battle. It could have been ten minutes or even a half an hour.

We turned the corner when I realized that Nick's breathing had changed. I had noticed it before, how loud it was compared to mine and Eli's. Now his breathing had gone ragged.

I turned and saw Nick holding his hand to his stomach. As I watched he fell to his knees. He fell against the marble wall and rested his head against the surface.

"Nick-" that's when I saw it, a red spot began to show on his suit. "Nick, what happened?"

Nick didn't answer, instead he closed his eyes shut and moaned softly.

Eli turned around and gasped at the dark red blood that began to grow more and more on Nick's suit.

I fell to my knees taking out the medical kit from the back of my suit. I looked around inside of it, trying to find the right supplies.

"It looks like he was shot." Eli responded after he got his breath back. There was panic in his voice. When I looked up at him I could see that his face was a pale white.

"It's okay," Nick barely managed out, "I'll be fine."

One look into his dark eyes told me the opposite. He was in pain, and a lot of it.

I looked down the hall. We were so close to reaching the creature's leader, so close. As if reading my thoughts Eli spoke. His voice was strong.

"You go ahead," he nodded at where the creatures had disappeared, "I can stay with Nick. I will take care of him. We will be fine, I promise." His voice was so certain. It was so strong that I almost believed him. Almost.

I got up. There was no way that I could turn down the offer. "Are you sure that you will be okay?"

Eli nodded, "Yes, I'm sure."

"Okay." I handed Eli the medical pack, "take care of him, alright?"

Eli nodded. His face was still pale but I could see a determined expression on his face. He would not let Nick die.

I took a deep breath. If I was going to do this alone I would need confidence and courage.

"Please be careful, Caleb." I felt an intake of breath. That was the first time one of my troops had called me by my name. I smiled.

"I will," I promised Eli, and then I turned and sprinted towards the creatures and towards their leader. I turned and sprinted towards saving the world.

The marble hallway continued on for a long way. I did not tire easily. I was trained for this moment. For this battle that would be exhausting, I was ready.

The white marble was very bright. It made you believe that it was never going to end. As I ran I felt like I was not moving at all. The white was so endless that it made me second guess my mind.

No wonder the creatures chose this tunnel. If they were

going to be followed they would know that humans would not be able to stand this tunnel easily. I continued forward though, there was too much at stake to not continue.

I could tell that I was nearing the end of the hallway. The crystal white marble hallway was changing. It was changing from white to a more grayish shade. The atmosphere was changing too. Instead of the thick air that made it feel like you couldn't breathe properly, the air thinned which made it difficult to breathe in a different way.

Finally the first turnoff of the hallway occurred. I stopped, if I chose the wrong hallway who knows where it would take me, definitely not to the creatures or to their leader.

"Think, Caleb, think." I said softly to myself. If I was a creature and I knew that I was being followed which hallway would I take?

I looked down each of the hallways. One was made of dirt and stone. It looked like it was a dead end and was very dark inside.

The other hallway was like the one before. It was bright and made of the marble material.

I thought back to what I knew about the creatures. They definitely did not like our Earth: it was dirty and rough. I could tell by the way they acted when they were inside it in the Resistance. Their eyes flickered around more so than usual and they had a nervous look about them.

If I was a human I would not think twice about which way to go and definitely go the way that I felt most comfortable with.

That is why we die. I thought to myself, we are too greedy for comfort. All we have to do is step outside of our limits and we will be saved. We will be… saved.

I started running again, I was sure of my decision. The creatures did not want to be like humans. They would do anything they could to do the opposite. As I continued running down the dirt-and stone-made hallway I smiled. This was the first step to outsmarting the creatures. This was my first step to saving the world.

"Caleb, Caleb, I did not think that you had the strength to come this far. I did not think that you had it in you."

I knew that voice all too well. It was the voice that still haunted me but it was the voice that encouraged me and the voice that helped to lead me onward even when I felt like all was lost.

I felt like my heart had been ripped out of my chest. Now, there was only a gaping hole where it should have been, there was an emptiness inside of me that did not feel like it could be replaced.

A creature that I recognized stepped forward. It was the leader of the creatures, the leader of the creatures, and… my father.

There was laughter that followed that sentence. A laugh that sounded full of life. I knew that it was a lie.

"Dad?" I barely managed out, "I… I thought that you were…"

"Dead?" he finished for me. There was humor in his voice, "No," he chuckled, "I am not dead. I am more alive than ever."

"What happened to you?" I asked softly, I could feel tears start to escape out of my eyes and pour down my cheeks.

My father acted like he didn't notice, "Well, I might as well tell you since we are going to change you anyways." He paused and looked at me. Then, he looked away again, "That night when there was a break in to the Resistance I did not die. Instead, I was only knocked out momentarily."

His words floated into my ears with ease but I was not hearing him. All I could do was stare at what had once been my father. All I could do was stare at the creature that I knew nothing about but used my father's body. All I could do was stare at the monster that plotted to overthrow mankind.

My father continued, "They brought me here, to my new home and my new life. It was here that I was changed. We call it The Change. It is where you go into the radiation chamber for a few days. When you come out, you are like us… creatures, as you like to call us. We prefer fast man. We will be the new generation of man, a generation without the greed and the hunger for power."

"Without greed and hunger for power?" I asked. I could hear the disbelief in my voice, "Then what are you doing now? You are trying to wipe out mankind for power, Dad, for power and greed only. There is no such thing as a generation of man with any amount of radiation that is not greedy or hungry for power." I paused, catching my breath. My father had a small smile on his face.

"You are just as I remember you, Caleb, always so interested in finding mistakes in every logical statement," he sighed, "You are going to be great as one of us, Caleb, you will a be great fast man."

"Wait," I said suddenly, realizing what he was saying, "you're human? I thought that creatures were… something else."

"Many of us are what you called bugs. When we are bugs for long enough we gradually evolve into what I am now. That is, unless you do what they did to me and put you in the radiation chamber…"

"Come on, Sir, get on with it." I looked around. For the first time I realized that I was surrounded by creatures. They must have stepped out of hiding while I was talking to my dad. I have to be more careful, I thought to myself. I always lose concentration when Dad is around.

I looked at the creature who spoke. He was holding a gun tightly. He looked very nervous and was dripping with sweat.

Most of the creatures that had surrounded me looked nervous. Their eyes flickered around in the darkness of the cave. They were in a place that they were not comfortable with. I could see that they wanted to get out of there, no matter the consequences. I clutched my cutlass tightly.

"Fine," my father spoke in a threatening voice. His lips curled up in a snarl afterward and the creature who spoke winced in fright.

"Are you the leader? The leader of the creatures, I mean, the leader of the fast man?"

"I am," my father responded, "and you will be once I die."

I took a deep breath. There was no way that I was going to join my father and the creatures to help destroy the world.

"I'm not joining you." There was harshness in my voice that I did not expect. Suddenly, anger flared up inside of me, anger that seemed out of my control. "I will never join you, not when you are like you are."

The sadness on my father's face looked sincere but I was not fooled, "I thought that you would act this way." He said. There was no sympathy in his voice. "That's why you don't have a choice."

"You're an animal." I said softly. I could not believe what was happening.

Anger replaced my father's previous expression, "Put him out," he ordered the other creatures, "but do not kill him."

The creatures started to advance on me. I tightened my grip on my cutlass. They did not attack at the same time which surprised me. The first one was an easy defeat. He circled me once then he lunged forward with quickness that I did not expect, I parried his blow and then took a swing at his right leg. He dodged it and attacked again but this time I was ready for the speed and swung sideways. As he was swinging I made contact and he fell.

This time two creatures advanced on me, they were prepared for my speed and were faster than me, but the fast men were not stronger. I was able to defend myself and patiently wait for the right moment to lash out and attack.

The supply of creatures seemed endless. They would keep coming as soon as I took others down. I would hope that they would stay down.

Suddenly, I heard nothing. The silence was so quiet that I could hear my ears buzzing. I looked around, thinking that all of the creatures were gone. Instead, I saw one creature left.

He was the creature that had spoke up to my father, I mean, the leader of the creatures. There was still sweat dripping down his face but his eyes looked determined, determined to put me out and get out of the tunnel.

He would get out of the tunnel at all costs. I could see his finger tense around the trigger. He would keep shooting as many times as needed to take me down, there was no getting around him. I stood there, waiting.

"You were a man once," I started speaking. I could not stop myself, "Remember the feelings of life that you had when you accomplished something big? Remember not having to hold back, do you remember what it feels like to be a man?"

The creature gulped. I could see that he was processing what I was saying. The creature was trying to figure out how to answer my question, trying to figure out if it was a trick.

Then the creature nodded slowly, "I do remember being a

man." He responded softly, "it was nothing like it feels now." The creature swallowed hard, I tried not to imagine what had happened to him.

The human that I had been seeing in the creature vanished. His eyes turned a darker shade of brown and glazed over. I knew that my battle had been lost.

The creature smiled hungrily, "But it feels so great to be a creature now." He laughed and tightened his grip on the gun.

This is it, I thought to myself. This is the end of my life as a human.

The sound of the gun going off was louder than I expected. I did not feel the pain but I knew that the pain would come soon.

I could feel myself drifting, drifting into a far away land that no one else knew about. But something was wrong.

"Caleb," I heard a voice in the back of my head, it was soft and smooth, it felt like I was falling asleep, "Caleb," the voice was louder this time, more persistent, "Caleb come on, let's go. We have to find the leader before it's too late."

I opened my eyes. The creature that was about to shoot me lay slumped in the corner. A large red spot was darkening in color on his chest.

His gun was across his lap and his legs and arms were all facing different directions that looked very uncomfortable and awkward.

I looked around, finally processing what I was seeing. I was not dead, I was not passed out. I was not a creature.

But then, who saved me?

Finally I realized, Eli.

I looked up into Eli's eyes. They still had the determined look that I had seen before on them.

"Eli, what… what happened?"

"I came looking for you. I knew that you needed help. But now is not the time, come on we have to move."

"But, Nick..."

"Nick is fine," Eli interrupted me, "Come on, Sir. We really should find the leader."

I shook my head back and forth, "I don't think that I can do it." I spoke slowly.

"What?" Eli asked, suddenly confused, "What do you mean?"

"The leader," I continued, "It's…it's my father."

"He's your father?" Eli asked. He looked confused, "I thought that you said that your father was… dead."

"I thought that he was," I could barely hear myself speak, "but he was only captured, they turned him. They turned him into a creature." I could hear the hatred in my voice.

Eli did not speak for a moment, but when he did it was soft but confident, "You can do it." He said slowly, "You got me to believe, and now I do. I believe in you, Caleb, I believe that you will do it and that you will be our hero… forever."

His words entered my body like a stream. They flowed in through my ears and down through my core and into my legs, the words circled back around until they reached my heart. I could feel the words bearing down on me. The words were so simple, yet so complex.

Could I do it? Could I defeat my own father?

"He's not your father anymore…" Eli was watching me, and for the second time today it seemed like he could read my thoughts, "now he's a creature. You said it yourself, they changed him."

He is not your father anymore. I replayed his words in my head. He is not your father anymore. He is not your father anymore.

He is not my father anymore.

"I can do it." I said softly. I believed it, I could do it.

CHAPTER 15

"When you can find yourself when all is lost, when you can keep control and use your mind to win, that is when you have the edge on your opponents, that is when you can truly beat them and do so under any circumstance."

My father was looking at me. It was the look that he gave when he expected me to do something. It was the look that he gave when he knew that you understood.

I nodded my head up and down slowly, showing him that I did understand and that I did want to learn from him.

"Do you believe in fairy tale endings?" Eli's question startled me back to consciousness. He was staring at the path ahead, his jaw was set.

"No," I said softly, "I don't." Eli did not move as I spoke but I could see his jaw tighten and stay rigid. "But I do believe in hard work and in trust. With those two things you can have happiness."

Eli nodded his head but his body was still tense and tight. I could tell that he was scared.

"What are you afraid of?" I asked. I was curious, I knew that it could be of the battle but something told me that it was something else.

Eli looked at me. His eyes met mine, but then looked away again. For a moment I did not think that he would answer.

"I am afraid of what will happen if we don't win. I am afraid of the outcome. What do you think they will do to us?"

They will kill us. I thought to myself, they want to create a world without humans, and that is just what they will do.

"I don't know." I answered Eli, that was not completely a lie, I did not know.

I thought about Grandfather and Justin. What would I do in a world without them? Then I thought about Jami. I thought about her laugh and the way she flipped her hair. I thought about her eyes, the way they looked just like the sea.

I could do this. I could defeat my father, if not for the world, for them. They would be saved.

We finally reached the end of the tunnel. There was one door. I knew that my father waited on the other side.

"You stay here." I heard myself say to Eli, "Make sure no one else comes in." Eli nodded and I believed him, he would do his job. I would have to do mine.

I took a deep breath and then opened the door and stepped out of the tunnel.

The room that I had stepped into looked familiar, too familiar, like I had been there already. There was a chair in the middle and no windows. The door that I entered from was the only door.

Then I remembered my dream. In the dream it was my father who had been sitting in the chair. When he woke up, he was like them, a creature.

This must be where they change the people into creatures. It is where my father led me. He expects that I will give in.

He was waiting for me.

"I knew that they would not be able to defeat you." His easy smile that looked too real was back, "so I decided to lead you here."

"I am not going to give in." I said. I could feel the anger in me start to build.

"No?" He asked. "We will see about that." He smiled as if he had just told me something sweet. Bitterness filled me on the inside.

"What did they do to you?" I spat out. I was angry at the creatures for turning my father into this creature. I wanted to strangle every last one of them, starting right here and right now, with my father.

"They made me into this."

He moved fast and I was not ready. Quickly, he closed the distance between us. As soon as he was close enough he grabbed me and threw me against the wall.

I could feel my body threaten to break on the impact. He was strong and fast.

"Do you really believe that you can defeat me, Caleb? Do you believe that you can overcome your emotions and fear of me to even come close? Why don't you join me? Together, we would rule the world."

"I would never join you, Father. There was a time that I would but not now. Not after the beast you have become."

My father laughed.

"Then what are you going to do? Hide?"

"No," I shook my head back and forth, "I'm going to defeat you."

The look on my father's face was pure disbelief. He was stunned at what I said. He was stunned that I was even considering defeating my father.

What he did not know was that I had my mind set. It was set on one thing only, save the world.

The battle lasted a long time. We were very evenly matched. He was very quick and strong but it seemed like he lost some skill during The Change. I did not think that the battle would ever end.

I was not going to give up and I doubted that my father would either. There was no rhythm to how father attacked so I was not going to be able to defeat him that way.

I could feel that we were both starting to lose strength. I could see him slowly weakening. His strength and quickness seemed to drop in intensity. The fire that had been in his green eyes was slowly dissipating.

I could tell that he was starting to get lazy as well. His swings had less strength. It was as if he was trying to conserve energy.

Also, his blocks seemed weaker. I was advancing on him. He was almost to a corner. I could feel the end of the battle approaching. All I had to do was corner him. Then, it would be over.

Suddenly, something changed. I could see the fire start up again in his eyes. It was strengthening. I could tell that some of his quickness was returning. He was getting stronger as well.

"You think for a moment that you can defeat me?" His words came out choppy and his breathing grew harder.

He threw back his sword and swung it forward with all of his strength. I was not ready for this move at all. The sword made contact with my cutlass but the speed and strength of the blow sent me flying backwards.

I landed hard on the floor at least five yards from where my father was. Now, he was advancing on me. I tried to get up to my feet but he stomped down on my chest hard and I felt all of the air inside of me leave my body.

"You will join me," My father said the words slowly, "and you will lead us to the fall of mankind."

After the long battle that had taken place I was tired. Very tired. I could feel my brain start to shut down. I could feel it closing on me. I could feel my body want to rest. I felt for one of the first times in my life… defeated.

But as my brain started to shut down I held onto the hope. I held on to the hope that I still could do it. I still could defeat my father. People were counting on me. Some people even believed in me.

I looked up into my father's eyes. They were not his eyes anymore. They were a creature's eyes. They were a creature's eyes that would do anything they could to find a way to defeat me. They were a creature's eyes that would rule the world once mankind was defeated.

Finally, I saw a way to win. My cutlass was lying on the ground behind my father. It was too far away to reach but I knew that if I could get to it I would be able to win the battle.

I grabbed my father's foot and with all of the strength that I had left in my body I threw his foot up into the air. My hope was that the momentum would keep going and my father would flip backwards onto his back. My father was strong and stood his ground but I was able to leap to my feet before he could put his foot back down.

"This is a mental battle now, Caleb." I heard my father say. He took a step towards me, and then another. I could tell that he was trying to gain ground on me. He was trying to break me. "I know your tricks and you know mine. Now, it is only mental toughness that will push one of us to victory. I think that we both know who will win now." My father smiled, "Join me now, Son, and you will have no pain to go through. Join me now and we will be able to fight together to win this war. Join me now and we will conquer the world."

Instead of answering, I sprinted towards my cutlass that was lying on the ground. I flicked it up with my foot and spun around.

My father was only watching me. There was a small smile on his face and his eyes sparkled. I remembered vaguely my father before he had been transformed into this creature. He looked a lot like he looked now. Maybe he still could be saved.

"Will you join me?" I asked softly.

My father was so taken by surprise that he faltered. He took a deep breath. Suddenly, he looked unsure of what to say.

"Will you join me?" I asked again. This time there was more urgency in my voice, "we would make a great team," I continued, "you and me?"

As soon as I spoke those words my father laughed and I saw the coldness return to his once bright green eyes.

I felt a heaviness settle over my heart. There really was no way to change him back. It was either I kill him or he defeats me and changes me into a creature where I have no sense of what I am doing.

He is not your father anymore, I heard Eli say in my head. *He does not know you like a father would. All he wants is to have the world to himself.*

I could do it. I could do it. I could save the world.

With renewed strength I was determined. My father was gone. A creature was simply using him. He would not want that. My real father would want to be put out of the state he was in right away.

I felt myself let my cutlass fly. I knew that as soon as I let go of it that it would hit its mark.

I did not want to watch, but I did. I watched my cutlass fly through the air. I watched as it pierced the heart of what used to be my father. I did not see my father fall. Instead, I saw only a creature fall. All I saw was a creature that only wanted me to quench his thirst of greed. All I saw was a creature that wanted to take out mankind.

As soon as my cutlass sank deep into his heart I saw all of the dark light drain from his eyes. He fell to the ground.

As soon as the creature hit the ground I fell to my knees. I could not believe what I had just done. I could not believe what I had just accomplished.

It is not over yet, I said to myself, there is still a battle going on outside. I felt myself get up to my feet.

I did not feel as I moved to the body of the creature I had just killed. I looked at the creature's face. It really was not my father. His eyes were a dark shade of brown. So brown that they almost looked black. Its hair was a dark black as well. This was not my father. This was not my father, it was only a creature. A creature with no regards for mankind. A creature with such greed that it wanted to wipe out a species.

I could feel a presence in the air. I could feel a presence that I often felt when something changed. I could feel the beast before I saw it.

The beast seemed to fall from the ceiling. I looked up from where I was standing. I was near the lead creature and saw it. Just by looking at its complex body I felt myself gasp in shock. The beast was huge.

It was the most horrifying creature that I ever saw. Dark scales rippled down its back and a long tongue with poisonous saliva lashed out every so often. Its head was large. It had a mane and sharp teeth. I could immediately tell that this beast was not like any beast that I had ever fought before, this one was larger. It was stronger. It was faster. This beast was mutated in three different ways instead of only two. I could tell that this beast was one of the newer species. This beast was one of the species that had gotten stronger.

Just by my first glance at the beast I could tell that it was hard to kill. I could not see any way for only me and my cutlass.

"Your leader is dead." I spoke to the beast slowly. The beast only growled and took a step forward.

I felt terror wash through me. I grabbed my cutlass from the creature's body and started backing towards the exit. While I was backing I never turned away from the beast. It was so huge that it already took up a large portion of the room.

The beast advanced towards me as I retreated. Its steps were long and covered the space between it and the lead creature in no time. At the lead creature the beast stopped moving. It looked down at the leader and then back up into the night, it howled in agony. It looked back at me. The beast's eyes were filled with hatred, but it did not attack. Then I knew. It did not know what to do. The lead creature was gone so it had no one to follow. It would not attack me or any of the other men. Now, it did not know how.

I felt my body relax. Slowly, I backed out of the room.

Eli was waiting for me. There was such fear on his face that I knew he had feared the worst. I could see that he was imagining the worst possible outcome. He was making it hard for himself to stay strong. He smiled when he saw me and threw his arms around me. I felt myself slowly start to smile as well.

We had completed our part of the mission.

"You did it," Eli said to me softly.

"Yes," I breathed out, "we completed our part of the mission. We did it."

I felt a small amount of relief wash over my troops when our craft took off into the night. Phillip said something to Eli which made Eli smile. I felt relief wash over myself as well. We had done our part. Hopefully, the other groups had done theirs.

I looked out of one of the windows of the craft. The world seemed so peaceful when you were flying by overhead. However, the trees were scarce. The few that were outside of the craft were beautiful.

I could see the sun start to appear over the horizon. The night was over, the night of the battle. The night of the war had ended and a new day had begun.

We reached the Resistance. There were people everywhere. Many crafts had already landed and fighters were piling out. Each of the fighters were giving each other compliments and laughing. There was joy again. There was joy that I had not seen at the Resistance for at least a week.

A hand grabbed my shoulder. I turned around.

"Justin," I said softly, when I saw the man's face. I pulled him into a hug, "I'm so glad that you are okay."

"Likewise, little bro, likewise," He looked at me, into my eyes, "Who was the lead creature anyways?" He asked.

I felt myself smile. He was not my father, not at all. Saying the truth felt great, "He was just another creature." I said to Justin. "He used our father's body to try and get me to join them. He was not our father."

I saw Justin think. He had his eyebrows furrowed.

I felt myself explaining everything to him. From the start of our journey, the flashbacks and the stress, to what my father had said, to The Change, the way that you could become mutated even if you were not before.

"They made our father become mutant." I heard myself saying to Justin, "I doubt he even really knew who I was. He was not our father anymore."

I saw Justin nod. Then, he pulled me into another hug. I felt myself smile again.

"I'm glad that you are okay, Caleb." Justin pulled away.

That's when I saw her, Jami. "I got to go," I told Justin. He was already gone. I walked up to her. I walked up to her as fast as I could. I weaved in and out of people rejoicing, never taking my eyes off of her.

When I reached her I lifted her high into the air. Then, I pulled her in to my body in a tight hug.

"You're okay." I breathed into her hair.

I heard her laugh, "We did it," she said softly, she looked into my eyes. There was a light in them that I had not seen before. The light was so bright that I was taken aback by surprise. Finally, she was happy.

A loud noise broke the happiness that filled the night. It was a low rumble that filled your body and made you feel like it was inside of you. It was one of those loud rumbles that seem to take up your body and lift you off of your feet, into the air.

Everyone started cheering when the large ship appeared. Instead of feeling happy by seeing the large ship I felt weird. It felt out of place beside all of the crafts.

"Is that General Johnson?" I asked Jami. I had to yell

loudly over the noise. She didn't answer. I looked down at her. Her face was a pale white. "Jami!" I grabbed her shoulders, forcing her to look at me. The ship had started its descent. "Jami, where is General Johnson?"

She looked into my eyes. There was fear in them that I had never seen before. "That is not who they think it is, Caleb." She looked up at the ship which was close to landing now.

"Who is it, Jami? Tell me!" Jami looked up into my eyes again. They were so blue, such a bright and beautiful blue.

"That's General Daniels. He has found us. I do not know how he did it."

I felt like all of the air had been taken out of my lungs. I ran my hand through my hair. General Daniels had wanted all of these people dead, what would he do now?

"We have to warn the people. We have to let them know." I turned away from Jami and faced the people. "Everybody listen up!" I yelled at them. No one could hear me over the cheers and shouts.

"Caleb, there is no use. Even if they do hear you they will not believe you." Jami grabbed my arm, "Come on, we have to find our siblings."

I let her pull me deeper into the crowd. Who would give away the location of our Resistance? Who would…?

"Wait, Jami." She turned to me, "where is General Johnson?"

I heard the ship land. All around us the cheering got even louder than before. I could barely hear myself think.

"Caleb, we have to find Phillip and Justin and get out of here now." I turned back to Jami. Her eyes were pleading.

"Alright, let's go."

Justin was not hard to find. He was in the middle of a group of his age men and women. They were laughing and talking. I grabbed his shoulder and spun him around.

"Hey, little bro," Justin spoke to me happily. There was a large smile on his face.

"Justin, we have to go."

"Sure, bro, sure," he waved carelessly to his friends, "I've gotta go, gentlemen. See you around ladies." He winked at one woman who giggled to her other lady friends, they all started laughing. Justin smiled.

I grabbed Justin and started hauling him out of the group. "Come on, Justin, we have to leave."

I grabbed Jami's hand and we took off again into the crowd. Now, we had to find Phillip. As soon as we made it back into the crowd I heard a noise. The door of the ship was opening. Instead of exhausted fighters filling out of the ship, troops, with guns raised and at the ready, came flying out. There were at least 50 of them and they started circling the group.

Almost immediately, the cheering stopped.

"What's going on?" I heard someone shout.

"Who are you guys?" Someone else asked. Chaos followed. People started scrambling to get away.

I squeezed Jami's hand hard and continued to search the crowd. A voice came across the night. It silenced the chaos immediately. I recognized the voice right away. It was the voice of the general. It was the voice of the general that had acted like a father to me for so many years. It was the voice of the general that had betrayed me. And it was the voice of the general that wanted the world to himself.

"There is no escape," his voice was hollow. He had aged a lot since I had last seen him. His hair was now gray and his eyes had little light in them. "I bet that you all are wondering who betrayed you." The general smiled.

Behind him, General Johnson stepped forward. I heard many people gasp. There were whimpers as well. He had been their general for years now. I could tell why many of them felt defeated.

I was not surprised by seeing General Johnson up there. He had always seemed very suspicious with his searching. Jami did not seem surprised either. She squeezed my hand tighter and continued forward.

I finally caught a glimpse of Phillip. Eli was with him and Nick was as well. I breathed a sigh of relief. They were all staring at the two generals on the ship. There was terror on their faces that I had not seen before now.

"Jami, over there," I pointed at where they were standing. Jami seemed to relax as well. I saw her tense shoulders loosen.

"Phillip," she called out softly, he turned and smiled when

he saw her he started making his way over to us. Eli and Nick followed.

"We have to get out of here now," I told them, "otherwise I am not sure what they are going to do with us." I took a deep breath, "follow us."

What the general said next took my breath away. I was so unprepared that I stopped walking.

"You all are probably wondering why we are here. I promise you all that we will not kill you unless you disobey our orders." The general smiled. His smile was laced with such lies and hate that I wanted to punch the smile off his face. "All you need to do is hand over Caleb Hanson to us. Then, none of you will die."

I did not hear what he was saying at first. I was busy scanning the crowd, looking for an escape. When Jami's hand squeezed mine, the general's words carried over to my ears. I felt myself freeze.

My hand ran through my hair. At first I did not think. I could not think. My brain stopped working for a moment as the general's words began to register in my mind.

Hand over Caleb Hanson to us. Then, none of you will die. Hand over Caleb Hanson. Thoughts began to enter into my mind.

Should I do it? Should I turn myself in and save everyone? But even if I did turn myself in I did not know if the generals would stick to their word.

Jami's hand squeezed mine even harder.

"You will not turn yourself in, Caleb. We look up to you, you are our leader." Her voice was pleading. I knew that it was more than what she said. Her blue eyes gazed into mine, "Please," she whispered, "Don't do it."

I looked at Eli, his face was white. He shook his head back and forth. He did not want me to do it either.

I looked at Phillip and Nick and Justin, they were all looking at me hard, "Don't do it, Caleb." Nick said. Phillip shook his head, agreeing with Nick.

Justin shook his head as well.

I looked up at the generals that were still standing on the ship. They were scanning the crowd. I could tell that they were trying to find movement.

Then I saw it. General Daniels was not a human. He was a creature, a fast man. They must have found him and turned him into one. He was very good at covering up. His movements were so slow and strained.

General Johnson must be a creature as well.

"They are creatures," I leaned down and whispered to Jami.

She looked up at me, her face was full of fear, "they can't be trusted, Caleb. They will not stay to their word."

"No?" The general asked, he seemed shocked, "none of you are going to turn him in?" He looked around. His eyes flickered so much, he was losing his cover. He definitely was a creature. "Every night there will be a killing. Every night three of your people will die until Caleb Hanson is turned in."

My destiny is saving people, I thought to myself. Could I save them in a different way?

"If we can kill both of the generals the creatures will not know what to do."

"What?" Jami asked.

"Eli hand me your gun." Eli did as he was told, he did not complain. Feeling his gun in my hand felt different. But I knew how to shoot a gun. I could hit a target from this far away. I had done it before.

I pulled the trigger of the gun. It seemed silent as it whistled through the night. It was going so fast I barely had time to think before it would hit its mark.

General Daniels saw the bullet coming. I knew that he did by the way his eyes traveled after the path of the bullet and by the way he moved. I could tell that he was ready. He leaned to the side and the bullet whistled by his head. He smiled.

Finding the path of the bullet through the early morning rays I knew that it would not be long until he found me. I looked up at the sun, it was about to appear on the horizon. It was so close to making its appearance.

The general's eyes met mine and he smiled. I knew that he recognized me. Even though he was a creature he still knew what I looked like. I remembered back to when I was a boy. It was when I first found out that my father had died battling the beast.

General Daniels had pulled me in tight to a hug. He told me that it would be okay. He told me that he would always be there for me. I felt comforted.

I remember believing him. He was the general of the biggest Resistance and I believed that every word he said would be true. Being a kid, I thought that generals would never lie. Being a kid, I believed that generals would always tell the truth and only the truth.

I remember trusting him. I remember always going to him for support and encouragement. He was my father then. That is what I called him, dad. Now he is only a creature, a creature that does not have any care except for himself.

I looked back up at the general. He was still smiling at me. He knew that I had been found and that there was no escaping now.

I felt Jami squeeze my hand. I looked down at her. Silent tears were rolling down her cheeks. She did not look at me. Her eyes were sharp. Their beautiful blue looked like waves in an ocean. Wonderful waves like no other. I just wanted to hold her close. I just wanted to tell her that everything was going to be okay.

Eli was crying as well. His eyes were red and tears were streaming down from them. His brown hair was ruffled by the wind.

Nick's breathing came out unsteady. In…out…in, out, in, out, in… There was no pattern. I could tell that he was scared of what would happen.

Phillip did not move. It was as if he could not believe what had just happened. He gazed up at the creatures on the ship with such hate in his blue eyes that I was taken aback by how mad he looked.

Justin was silent. He was looking at the sun that was still hiding behind the horizon. It would come up soon. I wanted to pull Justin into a hug. I wanted to hold onto him tight and never let go. I wanted to give him a hug one last time. The sun started to poke its head out of the horizon but Justin did not move. He only stood and stared. He stood and stared at what was going to be a beautiful day. He stared at what was going to keep us warm. He stared at the time that was ticking away for me.

I looked back up at General Daniels. He was still looking at me. It was an expression that seemed like he was eyeing me up. He was trying to figure out what I was going to do. Would I run? Would I fight back? He saw me looking at him and met my eyes. They were so dark, so lifeless that I was taken by surprise. I had no idea the loss of life that you received from becoming a creature, a creature that was greedy to have the world to themselves, and a creature that would take out anything in the way.

I did not hear him speak but I did see that his mouth moved he was saying my name. "Caleb." His eyes and hair fluttered in the cool breeze.

What no one on the ship or any of the humans on the land knew was that the bullet had hit its mark.

The sun finally showed its face. It was finally coming up over the horizon. During the time that it took to rise from below us it did not seem like anyone moved. Not even the birds sang out their tunes. They were ready for what was about to happen.

The explosion was so bright that even the sun's constant rays seemed to falter. I was ready for the explosion and tackled Jami and Eli to the ground. I hoped that everyone else would do the same.

The sound came next. It was so loud that many people screamed from the pain that it caused their ears. The boom sent pieces flying into the air.

I watched as the remains of the ship rained down all over the humans. The creatures, which were standing closest to the ship, were thrown into the air by the explosion. They crumpled into heaps on the ground beside the pieces of metal and parts of the ship.

As the pieces started to settle into place the humans got up and started cheering. They screamed at the tops of their lungs. These screams were of joy.

Slowly, I got up off of the ground. The cool air of what once was night washed over me. I turned to the sun, allowing it to warm my face. Its bright rays were now dominant again.

I felt a smile light up my face. Finally, I heard the birds start to chirp. Their songs sounded happy to my ears. I touched Jami's hand which was by my side. It was so smooth. I brought it to my mouth and kissed it softly. I smelt the pieces of burning rubble mixed with the sweet smell of grass and dew. Lastly, I tasted the warm air that entered my mouth and surrounded my skin. Finally, I felt happy.

Jami's soft voice brought me back to conciseness. "I can't believe that you just did that," she said softly, she shook her head back and forth, "you are amazing, I had thought that they were going to take you away. Now, I know never to give up hope on you." She laughed softly as she said those words.

I leaned down and kissed her hard. Her lips felt cool and sweet against mine. Finally I pulled away but I never let go of her hand.

I leaned into her again so that I could whisper in her ear. "I love you, Jami." Then I pulled away and stepped back.

I looked away before I could see her smile, and walked off before she could respond. I grabbed Eli and threw him up into the air, catching him before he hit the ground.

"You did it, Caleb!" He exclaimed happily. He started dancing in circles around me.

"We all did it." I replied.

I felt Justin pull me into a hug. It was so warm that I never wanted to let go.

"Good job, Bro." He said softly. He had a small smile on his face.

This is my destiny, I thought to myself, I can save, my destiny is to save. That is what I will do. I will continue to save and cherish what I have.

But my destiny is also something else, I thought to myself. I heard the laughter and felt the joy of finally winning. I felt the joy of the people around me. I felt the joy of the people that had been in hiding for so long. I could see the full sun in the sky now. It was so beautiful. The sun was full of such life and courage that it took my breath away.

The sun will always rise in the morning, I thought to myself. The sun will always begin a new day. The sun will always vanquish past worries. The sun will always save.

As I gazed up at the sun I realized that I also believed in something besides saving. I believed in something more. I believed in something that everyone should have the opportunity to do. I believed in something that should be a right.

My destiny is to live.

ABOUT THE AUTHOR

My name is Denali M. Pinto. I am 13 years old. I live in Boulder, CO. I love to play sports. I play many sports including basketball, volleyball, soccer, and tennis.

My favorite thing to do is be with my family. I love everyone in my family so much. They are all very awesome people and just being with them I have the best time in the world.

I have an awesome brother named Brody. He is such a cool guy. He plays all of my sports with me and pushes me to do my best. He is 11 years old.

I have been writing ever since I was very young. I think that I was in about 1st grade when I started writing. I have always loved to write fiction and I believe that I will continue to love to write fiction for the rest of my life. I am so excited about finishing this novel that I named Saved. It is a huge accomplishment for me.

I love how the main character, Caleb, always sets goals for himself. I believe that setting goals that will push you to achieve them is very important to live a full life.

I believe that when you have something to work for, or something that you believe in, you should not let anything or anyone stand in the way between you and your dream.

All in all, I had a great time writing the story. I had an amazing time developing the characters and creating an intense and good storyline. I am looking forward to continuing writing and hopefully creating many more novels to come.

Made in the USA
San Bernardino, CA
08 July 2014